EVER WORLD

LAND OF LOSS

K. A. APPLEGATE

SCHOLASTIC INC.
New York Toronto London Auckland Sydney
Mexico City New Delhi Hong Kong

For Michael
and Jake

No part of this publication may be reproduced in whole or in part, or stored in a retrieval system, or transmitted in any form or by any means, electronic, mechanical, photocopying, recording, or otherwise, without written permission of the publisher. For information regarding permission, write to Scholastic Inc., Attention: Permissions Department, 555 Broadway, New York, NY 10012.

ISBN 0-590-87751-8

12 11 10 9 8 7 6 5 4 3 2 1   9/9 0 1 2 3 4/0

Printed in the U.S.A.

First Scholastic printing, July 1999

CHAPTER

I

In the real world the Vikings never fought the Aztecs.

This was not the real world.

I had a sword in my hand. My fingers were so tight around the hilt that blood was seeping from my cuticles.

My breath came in shallow gasps. So little air I should have passed out. Knew I should breathe but couldn't, couldn't make my chest relax enough, couldn't unknot my stomach to let the air come in.

My body was a series of vises, vises on vises, all twisted tight, tight till the bones cracked and sinews and muscle screamed.

I was running. Legs stiff, like a puppet. It probably looked funny. Big, bounding, awkward steps with knees that alternately locked and collapsed.

Widen out the picture and I was just one scared fool in a mass of thousands. They were all around me, ahead of me, behind me, on either side. Big, bearded, indifferently armored, helmeted, ax-swinging, sword-waving, screaming, yelling, running, running and falling and climbing up to charge again, always yelling at the top of their harsh voices.

Up the beach. Over warm sand. Feet losing three inches of slide with every step. Sand sucking at you, trying to stop you, trying to keep you from this suicidal rush. But all around was the madness. Men in the lunatic rage of combat. Hungry for murder. Thirsty for the blood that would drench the sand. Not their own, of course, never their own, because what fool ever goes to war expecting that he will be the one to die? The movie in your head has you as the hero, bravely whacking away at the bad guys. Courage without the sight of your own intestines spilled out in the buttery sunlight.

That wasn't my movie. I'm not a romantic.

I ran. David ran. He was beside me, a few feet away; we wobbled one way or the other, back and forth, nearer and farther. On David's right, hanging back, sensible person that he was: Jalil.

April? Back on the boats. Back on the Viking

longboats that had been beached like so many confused whales all down the strand.

She had a pass. She was a girl. She had a uterus, so she didn't have to fight, couldn't, not according to the Vikings. So she was on the boat. Safe? Not if we lost. But if we won, yeah, safe, out of it, sipping bad Viking ale and eating roasted lamb and watching us as if she were in a skybox at the Super Bowl, thinking what damned fools we were.

If I'd had room in my head for any emotion beside fear I'd have felt jealous. But fear was filling every wrinkle and knob of my brain. Fear soaked through the gray matter that at other times concerned itself with passing tests and getting girls and avoiding speeding tickets and coming up with clever one-liners that made everyone laugh.

Ah-hah-hah, that Christopher is so funny. Man, he's funny. I mean, he really is.

That's me, funny, funny, Christopher.

Want to know what's funny? Funny is a high-school junior surrounded by sweat-reeking wild men, waving a sword and rushing at a bunch of Aztecs. That's funny.

Aztecs. Mexica. Those were their official names. Flesh-eaters. Blood-drinkers. Man-burners. Heart-thieves. The Vikings have all kinds of names for them. The Vikings think the Aztecs are a bunch of crazed psycho killers in the service of an evil god. And it's not like the Vikings are a bunch of Altar Guild Ladies from the local Baptist church.

The Aztecs were ahead of us, in a line. They looked ludicrous.

They wore feather headdresses, they disguised themselves as eagles, they disguised themselves as jaguars, they carried shields made out of sticks. Their swords looked vicious enough, like the snouts of sawfishes. But then you realized they were just hardwood with sharp chips of black rock embedded in the edge. Not much use against a steel sword, even the rusty, dented, tin-can things the Vikings use.

But the Aztecs had another weapon: short spears they flung with the aid of a notched stick. We'd been warned about those.

So that's where I was. Running toward a solid wall of Aztecs on a mission to chop off the head of their god Huitzilopoctli and bring it back to Loki so that he'd free Odin.

"Makes perfect sense," I muttered through chattering teeth, bounding stiffly, sliding and trying to keep from falling on my own sword.

Suddenly, from down the line, the big black Viking king named Olaf Ironfoot started yelling, "Mjolnir! Mjolnir!"

We hit the Aztec line. Two lines of men slammed together, literally, physically, so that you could hear shields grinding on shields and chests against chests and swords and axes all flailing wildly.

I was behind David. Some Aztec swung at him. David ducked. Then he drove his own sword into the feathered man and lurched away.

The Aztec fell. Not dead. Yet. But with blood and something black coming through the hands that clawed at his belly.

There was a sound coming from me, a noise, a moan, like a wounded animal, repetitive, wordless. Coming out of my throat and me having no control, no choice but to make that sound.

I was muscled aside by Thorolf, a Viking who'd taken charge of us. Thorolf was yelling, bellowing, roaring, swinging the big ax he carried up over his head and bringing it down like he was Abe Lincoln splitting rails.

I was down!

Sand in my mouth. Wind knocked out of me.

What had happened? Was I cut? Was I hurt? I dropped my sword, rolled onto my back, slapped myself frantically with my hand, looking for the wound. Couldn't see. Something in my eyes.

Blood!

I'd been hit in the head. Was I dying?

Feet stamped the sand all around me. A kick. I rolled over on my side. Dizzy. Wiped the blood out of my eyes. Fingers grazed a cut on my scalp.

Sickness washed over me as I realized I had just touched my own skull.

I'd never seen what hit me. And now I was in the rear, the Vikings pushing on, pushing the Aztecs back. Steel weapons versus obsidian and wood and bone.

"Mjolnir! Mjolnir!" the Vikings bellowed till it became a constant background roar, loud as a CTA train rushing by, almost drowning out the cries of rage and pain.

Mjolnir. The hammer of Thor.

The Aztecs were on the run! Back toward the tall, golden walls of the city they called New Tenochtitlan. Back toward the distant, stepped pyramid that towered above those walls.

I made it to my feet, tripped, staggered, caught myself, stopped, and went back for my sword. Blood was in my eyes again, my hand so wet with it that I couldn't clear my vision.

"Mjolnir! Mjolnir!"

David was gone. Jalil, barely visible, just his head, surrounded by Vikings twice his size.

Could I go back to the boats? I was injured, wasn't I?

Then I saw a Viking, an Asian guy, with a short, obsidian throwing spear sticking out of his upper thigh. He was staggering forward, yelling like all the others.

"Guess not," I muttered.

Besides, we were winning. The Aztecs were on the run. And as long as I didn't run too fast I probably wouldn't catch them.

I saw a flash of David. Just his head. He was stopped. Staring.

And through the Vikings, like an ice-cold wind, the terror blew.

The cries of "Mjolnir!" died away, replaced by the low, animal moan that men make when they are afraid, deep-down-inside afraid. I knew that sound. I'd been making that sound.

I'm tall. Taller than David or Jalil. Not as tall as a lot of the Vikings, but tall enough that from the back of the mob, standing on a slight rise in the sand, I could see the pyramid.

It was impossibly, absurdly high. Like it had been drawn by an artist with no sense of perspective.

Atop the pyramid, on the flat platform, was a temple. An open building on the front side and yet dark within, despite the bright morning sun.

From that temple stepped a creature out of a

madman's nightmares. He was huge! Almost as tall as the temple itself, and somehow, in defiance of all logic, his shadow fell across us.

We must have been half a mile away, but his shadow fell across us, across me, the darkness, the cold reaching deep inside me.

He was mostly blue, with broad, horizontal yellow stripes across his face. The blue was the blue of a late afternoon sky. The yellow was the yellow of unpolished gold. There were burning stars in his eyes, a burning mirror in one hand, a monstrous green snake in the other.

Huitzilopoctli. Aztec god.

We had come, armed with Mjolnir, to cut off his head and deliver it to Loki.

"Not happening," I said.

Huitzilopoctli grew wings, fabulous rainbow wings that spread wider than a thousand eagles.

He flew from the top of the pyramid and swooped down toward us.

Impossible, of course. Nothing that big could fly. It violated the laws of physics, that's what Jalil would have said.

Impossible anywhere in the universe.

Only, this wasn't the universe.

This was Everworld.

CHAPTER
II

Everworld.

Somehow, someway, for some reason, the old gods of Earth decided to abandon the real world. We didn't know why. Just knew that the gods of the Norsemen and the gods of the Greeks and the gods of the Aztecs and the Inca and the Egyptians and all the endless panoply of immortals, all decided they'd had enough of the real world. Our world.

They moved. They built themselves a little space-time condo. A separate universe.

They brought all the creatures of myth and legend. And they dragged a healthy number of humans across with them, because, hey, what's the point in being a god if there's no one around to kiss your immortal butt?

For a while, I guess, everything was fine. I have to guess because I don't know. I don't know much.

But somehow, into this combination Asgard-Olympus-Boca Raton, this cosmic retirement home for gods of war and love and wine and mischief and death — and no doubt pizza, for all I know — strangers crashed the party.

Immortals. Gods. But not human gods.

Then all hell broke loose. And now, somehow, don't ask me, there was some god-eating god from some dark armpit of the galaxy who was scaring the eternal pee out of the human gods.

Ka Anor. Not a nice creature. So I gathered from the fact that Loki, who isn't exactly a cheerleader himself, is scared by him.

Why was I there? Because of a girl named Senna.

Senna Wales. A freaky piece of work, but with a B-plus face and an A-plus body, assuming you're not one of those guys looking for eight pounds of silicone. Smart. Weird. Sexy. Inscrutable.

Man, I was hot for her.

Then it all went sour. Don't know why. She was like a spider who'd wrapped me up in the silk web and was ready to finish me off, and me wanting to be finished off, and then, nothing.

Next I see her, she's with David.

And yet, I was there that too-early morning, down by Lake Michigan, called there by a voice that only my deepest brain heard. I was down there watching, me along with Jalil and April and David, when the world went "tilt."

A wolf the size of a tractor trailer broke through from somewhere that was definitely not a suburb of Chicago. Broke the barrier of our comfy, cozy little universe and snatched up Senna in his jaws.

We were dragged along in the backwash.

Next thing we know, Senna's gone, we're face-to-face with a pissed-off Loki and a bunch of trolls, and Loki wants to know what we've done with "his witch." Senna.

Long story short, we escaped and got in tight with some Vikings who were about to leave on a mission for Loki. A mission to kill Huitzilopoctli and bring his head home as a trade-in for the freedom of Odin One-Eye, boss god of the Norsemen.

And it gets weirder. Because we aren't all the way into Everworld. We're there as long as we're awake. Go to sleep and we slip back into our old lives in the real world.

In and out. Back and forth. Cutting assembly

and groaning about the homework and checking
out the visible panty lines one minute, being
chased by murderous trolls the next.

It's a lunatic life.

Dangerous, too.

CHAPTER

III

Huitzilopoctli flew, swooped down on us like a gigantic bird of prey, and the Vikings fell back.

Instead of looking ahead to see backs, I was seeing faces now. Worried, frightened, disheartened faces. It wasn't a stampede. More like a hand that had reached out and touched a hot stove and yanked back almost instinctively.

The Big H looked like any one of his warriors. More feathers. Larger. And blue, of course. But it wasn't what you saw of Huitzilopoctli that scared you. It was what you felt.

There are people you meet, people whose eyes you happen to look into and right away you know. You know that they are apart from the basic humanity that more or less unites us. You know, without knowing why, that you're seeing a person whose pleasure comes from the pain of others, someone whose entertainment is gloating at the terror of others.

Beneath the shadow of Huitzilopoctli's wings you didn't have to look at him to feel the evil. It invaded your mind. Like an acid, it ate away your defenses and seeped into your soul.

I started to run. A hand grabbed me.

David.

"We can't run," he gasped, looking feverish and wild.

"Why not?"

"It's what *she* wants," he said.

She? I said something like "forget you," only several shades more intense. I didn't know who *she* was. I didn't care. I tore loose of his grip. A big Viking slammed into me, knocked me down on my back, and kept on running.

The Aztecs, emboldened by their god, counterattacked. They made a weird, trilling scream as they came on.

I tried to stand up. Too many fleeing bodies all around me. Legs, knees, feet hitting me, heedless. My head was still bleeding.

David grabbed me again. Crouched next to me. We were a boulder in a stream.

"I think she's with him!" David hissed. "Senna! She's with Huitzilopoctli!"

"I don't give a damn!" I yelled.

"Stand fast with Mjolnir!" Olaf Ironfoot bellowed, suddenly now just a spear's throw away. "Mjolnir!"

"We still have the hammer!" David said.

"Are you nuts?!" I shrieked. I told him where he could stick Mjolnir.

"If we go for the boats they'll cut us to pieces," David said. "We won't be able to get the boats off the beach, and if we try we'll be exposed and helpless. They'll have us by the rear. We have to hold our ground!"

Somehow that calm, cool assessment, that military judgment penetrated my panic. He was right. We couldn't run for the boats, the Aztecs would be all over us. They'd massacre us at their leisure.

I let David yank me to my feet.

"Come on!" he cried fiercely.

The glory-hog moron. Like the two of us were going to turn this disaster around.

I pushed David aside, sucked in the first real breath I'd taken in twenty minutes, and yelled, "Are the Vikings all women? Are you all cowards?"

That little insult slowed approximately no one. Not one of the big men said, "Hey, he's right, what are we, a bunch of wussies?"

They kept right on past. I could see the Aztecs

rushing toward us. They were smiling. Smiling and waving their Stone Age weapons up at their lunatic god, who swooped low, spreading his own private cloud of doom in his wake.

"The song!" David yelled. "Give them the song!"

I knew which song. The Vikings believed we were minstrels. We'd obliged them by coming up with a song that just made them crazy.

I looked at David and actually laughed. It was a sad, barking little laugh of despair, but it was a laugh.

He was right. You can't retreat with nothing but ocean and the mouth of a river behind you. We had to win this battle. Or die.

"Mine eyes have seen the glory of the mighty Viking lords!" I croaked in a harsh voice that would have gotten me ejected from a middle-school talent show.

"They are trampling out the vineyards where the grapes of wrath are stored. They have loosed the fateful lightning of their terrible swift swords, the Vikes are marching on!"

David had joined in, too. And man, were we pathetic. Like ants putting on a show of defiance just as someone's lowering a size-thirteen Ecco boot on them.

And yet . . .

And yet, about three Vikings slowed down. Thorolf was among them. Jalil was with him.

"Sing, Jalil!" I said.

We sang, the three of us. The Aztecs rushed on. The Vikings kept running. Only not as fast.

For a long, horrible moment the battle hung in the balance, hung poised on the edge of a rout and slaughter.

The ragged Aztec line was rushing. The Viking line was pulling back.

In the few yards of no-man's-land that separated the two armies stood Olaf Ironfoot. All alone. Just him and Thor's hammer

About ten feet behind him was our little knot composed of three quivering teenagers and a handful of Vikings all yelling a mangled version of the "Battle Hymn of the Republic."

And swooshing by overhead like some kind of gigantic, satanic piñata, the feathered Aztec god who lived on human hearts.

We sang, because we were dead meat and we'd have tried anything, anything to stay alive for another eight seconds.

"We jumped aboard our longships and we sailed upon the seas, and —"

Suddenly, a new voice chimed in. Big Olaf and

his big baritone. He threw back his head and yelled the words up at Huitzilopoctli while he brandished Thor's hammer.

"— and we slaughtered all who fought us and we did just as we please, 'cause we're crazy Viking warriors and we never beg for peace, the Vikes are marching on!"

People do strange stuff in battle. You take a human and pump him full of adrenaline and, in the case of the Vikings, a lot of beer, and you never know what's going to happen.

The Vikings stopped running.

We sang and they stopped running. They turned. They hesitated. Then Sven Swordeater, a kid not much older than me, yelled in his muffled, mangled speech, "Follow me!"

And all down the line of battle other Viking lords yelled, "Follow me!" And the line surged back up the beach, back toward the Aztecs.

Olaf exploded in insane laughter. He drew back his arm and let fly with Mjolnir.

The hammer flew. The stubby little handle and the cinder block of steel flew. Up and up, farther, faster, harder than was possible. I mean, it was like that hammer had a rocket backpack.

Mjolnir flew toward Huitzilopoctli.

CHAPTER

IV

Huitzilopoctli carried no weapons, at least not in the conventional sense. In one hand he had a sort of smoking mirror. It was round, like a discus or a squashed Frisbee. It was maybe ten feet in diameter.

In his other hand was a snake. The snake was a brilliant, shocking green. The snake wrapped back over Huitzilopoctli's shoulder. Its tail disappeared in the god's iridescent feathers.

Mjolnir flew. Every head craned back to watch it. Every eye, Viking and Aztec, watched.

There was a sound like a thousand-pound bullet slamming into a million pounds of raw beef.

Mjolnir hit Huitzilopoctli in his left arm. Hit him just above the elbow. The hammer broke through flesh, shattered bone, ripped the arm off, and sent it spinning slowly through the air.

Ten thousand voices wailed.

The arm, as long and thick as a subway car, fell. The Aztecs beneath it scattered. But it's tough to run in sand.

The arm landed with a terrific impact that sent shock waves to weaken knees and ruffle hair. A dozen Aztec warriors lay crushed.

And let me tell you, this wasn't some fake, unreal arm. Huitzilopoctli may have been a god, but I saw splintered white bone, as thick as an old oak tree.

Mjolnir inscribed an arc through the sky, then came racing back to Olaf's waiting hand.

The Vikings roared.

The Aztecs wailed.

Huitzilopoctli said nothing. He swooped around, slowed, then, as both Vikings and Aztecs fell back, making room, he landed. Just stopped flying, put down his legs, and landed. He was about the height of a five- or six-story building. Maybe ten times as tall as Olaf. Fifty times taller than me because I was hugging the sand now.

One huge, sandaled foot planted itself just a few dozen feet away.

Jalil's face was in the dirt beside mine. He shot me a look. "We can hurt the foot," he said.

I assumed he was babbling. But David was nodding agreement.

The Aztec god's big toe was as big as all of me. But yeah, a sword would hurt it. Had to hurt.

"Who are you, human, that you come to trouble me?" a voice demanded. A huge, rolling voice devoid of emotion, devoid of even the possibility of emotion.

Olaf looked nervous. He spoke up bravely enough but he sounded like a Chihuahua yapping at a tank. "I am Olaf Ironfoot!"

"Who sends you against me?"

"I come to free Odin One-Eye from unjust captivity in the dungeons of Loki!"

I don't know if Huitzilopoctli was stumped by this or thought it all made perfect sense. I couldn't see his blue-and-gold face. Couldn't see the burning supernova eyes.

"You have a brave heart," Huitzilopoctli said. The word "heart" sounded like an obscenity.

The snake on his shoulder lunged, quicker than any human eye could follow.

The green fangs closed around Mjolnir.

Olaf jerked the hammer back and tried to swing. But the windup was short. His arm was being blocked by the snake. Mjolnir flew, but ineffectually.

The magic hammer circled back to Olaf's hand.

Huitzilopoctli threw the smoking mirror. Like a Frisbee. It skimmed out and then, just like Mjolnir, circled back, spinning at impossible speed just a few feet above the sand.

Olaf jumped. Straight up. A high jump.

Not high enough. The mirror sliced off Olaf's one real foot. It clanged against the iron foot. It careened off, still spinning, and into the Viking ranks.

The deadly, ten-foot-wide disc sliced men in two. I don't know how many men. A lot.

Sven Swordeater was sliced in half, right at the belt. The top of his body slumped to the sand. His legs remained standing. He landed on his side. I could see him staring at his still-standing legs.

Olaf was on his back. Crippled. He threw Mjolnir but the throw was weak and wild. It flew past Huitzilopoctli's head, ruffling a few bright red feathers.

The Aztec god reached down with his good hand.

"Now!!" David cried.

He was up, I was up, Jalil was up, Thorolf was up, all of us running madly for the near foot.

I got there first. I held my sword stabbing-style, drew it up, arched my back, and down, down, down! The point sliced into the foot. Thorolf's ax, David's sword, and Jalil's all bit deep.

Nothing!

No blood, no cry of pain, no agonized reflex.

Huitzilopoctli lifted a helpless Olaf Ironfoot off the sand. He held him by the legs and used the jaws of the snake to hold the top half.

He broke Olaf in half and swallowed the king's still-beating heart.

CHAPTER
V

The Vikings broke and ran. No good. As David had predicted, they were caught trying to shove the boats off the beach.

I don't know how many died in the massacre that followed. Thousands, I guess. I don't know how many were taken prisoner. I was. David was. Jalil? April? We had no way of knowing in the mad chaos.

It took all the rest of the morning and into the afternoon for the Aztecs to round everyone up. Meanwhile, we sat in the sand. No food. No water. Hot, with the slowly sinking sun blistering the open wound on my head.

Finally, with evening coming on, they marched us into New Tenochtitlan in columns, armed Aztecs all around us. We stumbled with the weariness of the defeated through huge gates, onto streets laid out and cobblestoned with mathematical precision.

Women and kids came out of the houses to taunt us. Throw things at us: ashes from the fireplace. Bones. Feces. It wasn't pretty.

I tried to look around and see if I could spot Jalil or April. I hadn't seen either of them. But it was a sea of heads, big, tall Vikings with their heads down, but still tall enough to screen Jalil or April.

David was beside me. He was looking around, too. Looking for a way out. David, the insecure hero-wanna-be. This was all some kind of macho party for him.

Me? I wanted out, too. But I wanted out of it all. I was done with Everworld. I was ready to go home, stay home, sit in my desk at school and do my homework and take my quizzes and call the teachers "Sir" and "Ma'am" and rush straight home to tell my mom I loved her and tell my dad he was my hero.

That was the direction of my escape: home. The real world.

But David was busy sizing up the walls and the defenses and the proud, happy, cocky Aztec warriors.

Down along broad avenues we trudged. Neat, spotlessly clean adobe and stone buildings rose on either side of us. Businesses, I suppose, shops. And some houses. Some of the buildings were three stories high. All were crowned by deliriously happy Aztecs waving palm branches and throwing poop.

"They don't throw food," a voice said.

I jerked my head around.

"Jalil! Where have you been? David, Jalil's here, man. Didn't see you, where were you?"

"Hanging back," he said calmly. "I wanted to see if you guys were in any special trouble first."

That kind of annoyed me. But this wasn't the time to complain about Jalil's tendency to look out for himself.

"I don't see anything yet," David muttered. "But you know, they'll probably party all night. Get faced, pass out, maybe get careless . . ." He dodged a flying turd. He dodged. I didn't.

"They aren't throwing food," Jalil said again.

"You were hoping for watermelon and fried chicken?" I snapped as I wiped the stuff off with my sleeve.

"You know, you turn into a real redneck when you get stressed," Jalil said with a smirk.

"What about food?" David asked. "So what?"

"So, if you're looking to pelt the losing army with stuff, you go and dig out the garbage, right?

You hit them with apple cores and . . ." — he rolled his eyes toward me — ". . . chicken bones and watermelon rinds. But these folks aren't throwing food. Not even scraps. And look at them. The civilians, I mean."

I looked. Looked more closely, I mean.

"Skinny," I said.

"Malnourished," Jalil said. "Borderline starvation. The soldiers are well-fed, but the kids and the women are not. Plus, do you see any old folks?"

I didn't. And I didn't like where Jalil was going.

"Huitzilopoctli eats the hearts. Who eats the rest?" Jalil asked.

It was bad walking through a crowd of people who looked at you as an evil invader.

It was worse walking through people who looked at you as lunch.

They walked us past the base of the mountainously tall pyramid. Huitzilopoctli was nowhere in sight.

The pyramid reeked. The stench was intolerable. It made you hold your breath.

It wasn't hard to guess the source of the smell. The steps of the pyramid, from top to bottom, were covered with a dried crust many inches thick.

Blood.

I looked up those stairs and imagined how much blood it would take, and how quickly it would have to be spilled, for it to run all the way down from those heights.

I wanted to go home. I wanted that very badly.

"Well, this isn't all that bad," I said. It was an hour later. We, that is to say me, David, Jalil, and about two thousand of our closest Viking friends, were all locked in an enormous room. The ceiling was maybe twenty feet over our heads. The walls so far away they'd have been a ten-minute walk. Massive pillars, each as big around as a sequoia, held up the ceiling.

Up there, interspersed between pillars, were grates to let in air and light. The light was fading fast. It was already as dark as my basement at home. People walked across the grates. Probably stopped and looked down at us. I couldn't really tell.

The Aztecs were better builders than the Vikings. That was for sure. The Vikings were at the log and straw stage pretty much. The Aztecs were into the great big Toyota-sized stones form of building.

And the Aztecs cared about the simple things in life. Recessed into one wall were a series of stone cubicles with toilets. You did your business, yanked a chain, and they flushed.

And they had baths. Centered in the vast hall, low-slung square vats of warmish water.

The Vikings, naturally, had no interest in the baths.

I guess no one in that room had much interest in anything. The Vikings were quiet. None of their usual boisterousness. None of their bragging. No one calling for a poem or a song or a tankard of ale. No one threatening to split anyone open with an ax.

Just glum, downcast faces. Not surprising. Everyone knew. Everyone knew what was coming for us. Didn't know when, but we knew we were going to be marched up the stairs of that pyramid, where the priests would stretch us back over the stone altar and expertly cut out our hearts while our blood ran rippling down the steps.

Couldn't think about that. Couldn't. It made my stomach heave, my heart miss, my throat clench.

"Wouldn't mind washing the crap off my head," Jalil said.

I breathed. I'd stopped when that hideous image popped into my head.

I held out a hand, palm up, inviting. "Go for it. Doesn't look like there's going to be a fight over the hot water."

Jalil looked nervous. So did David.

"Locker-room willies all over again, huh?" I mocked them. "Afraid the big, mean Vikings will laugh at your . . . equipment?"

"It's a jail," Jalil said. "You realize that, right? No women? Bunch of guys looking for the weak ones so they can . . ."

"I'm not sitting here with crap smeared all over me," I said. "I'm taking a bath."

It was a small expression of courage. But I needed to do something besides sit there and imagine what it would feel like to live for those last few seconds staring up at my still-beating heart.

Like Sven Swordeater had gaped stupidly at his own legs.

Like . . .

Breathe. Breathe. Don't show the fear.

"I'd prefer a shower," I said, trying unsuccessfully to sound nonchalant. "I've never been a bath person. But I guess I'll make do."

I began to strip off my clothes. The Norsemen did not seem especially fascinated. One glanced up, I suppose to see if, as an outlander, I had something unusual, say a tail.

Naked, I climbed up into the bath. I settled in slowly because right about then it occurred to me that the baths might not be baths.

But no, my bare feet found smooth stone. The water rose around me as I shivered down into it. There was something semiliquid, like melted wax, in a woven-leaf dish. I stuck a finger in and smelled.

"Soap," I said. "Kind of flowery, but it's soap." I began to carefully wash the matted gash on my head. I didn't have any Bactine but I could at least get it clean.

"What do you do?" the curious Viking asked gruffly.

"I'm taking a bath."

He shook his head. "Your comedies will not lift many hearts today, friend minstrel."

I scooped up some of the mango-smelling goo and lathered it into my hair. Jalil was next to climb in. Then David. Three all-American kids with a lifetime of soap and deodorant jingles playing in their heads. We were in the third circle of hell, but determined not to smell bad.

I lay back and closed my eyes. I knew I wasn't ready to sleep. But I could lay back and think of something other than the horror I'd seen that day.

I could think about lying on the couch, watching the tube. I could think about playing tag football in the park down by the lake, using the pull-up bar as a goalpost. I could think about me and a few buds catching the train and heading down to Chicago on a hot summer day and wandering around Navy Pier with our shirts off, looking for girls, looking for fun, looking for trouble.

I could think about something besides the impossible monster that would soon be feasting on my heart.

No. I couldn't. I couldn't think of anything but that. Nothing but pictures of the brutality I'd witnessed. And the things that might have happened or even be happening to April.

Had Senna known? When she dragged us into this, had she known what it would be like? Had she known she'd be dragging her half sister into this? Me, Okay. Senna and I were done, but what about April? They lived together, for God's sake.

I opened my eyes and looked around. David was deep in thought. Jalil, too.

I wanted to ask them. They wouldn't know the answer, but didn't we have to at least think about it? Ask ourselves what we were doing there? Jalil would at least have some kind of theory. Something more profound than my own simple belief that we were screwed, screwed, utterly, irretrievably screwed by Senna Wales.

"So how do we get out of here?" David wondered, his head pinkish-white with lather.

"On a plate, surrounded by potatoes and carrots," I said.

He shot me a dirty look. "How do we get out of here?" he repeated.

Jalil looked blank. I looked blank. I was tired. Exhausted. The warm water made me want to sleep. To sleep was to escape back to the real world.

"We have more than a thousand of the toughest warriors anyone ever saw," David said, looking around at the Norsemen.

"We have squat," Jalil said. "They don't work for us. We're minstrels, remember? No one promoted us to generals."

"Hope April's okay," I said.

Stupid! Don't think about April again. Don't think about April. Don't picture what might be happening to her.

Breathe.

"She's probably okay," David said. "Her. And Senna."

I exploded. Don't know why, I just blew up. "Senna can die for all I care! Senna can be Big H's next meal for all I care! Forget Senna! She's the stupid head-case who got us all into this!"

Breathe. The vise was around my chest, squeez-ing the air out of my lungs, the blood out of my heart. I could feel my heart. It was right there, in my chest, under the ribs, under the breastbone, my God, they would split me open like a chicken, chop through the cartilage, my heart, beating, ar-teries pulsing, the blade, the serrated obsidian blade would sever the veins and arteries and my heart would . . .

I would scream. I would scream and beg and they wouldn't care, wouldn't hesitate, I was noth-ing to them, nothing to the blood-crazed god who would eat my heart.

Breathe. Breathe.

Breathe.

"Okay, look," David said in a low voice. "It's bad. As bad as it can be. But we have to deal with it as well as we can. There has to be a way out. Has to be."

Jalil laughed with no trace of humor. "David, the blood on that pyramid? Tens of thousands of people have gone up there to lose that much blood. Tens of thousands. Maybe hundreds of thousands. They probably all thought there was a way out."

I climbed out of the tub.

Breathe, Christopher. Breathe.

Chapter VII

Driving up the middle, shirt off, ball bouncing up to imprint its pebbly surface on my hand, Nikes slipping on the polished wood surface. A hand shot out, tried to snag the ball. No way. I shouldered him aside.

The basket right in front of me, wide-open . . .

Memory flooded my brain. Vikings. Aztecs. Olaf split open like a chicken, Sven sliced in half.

Huitzilopoctli.

I lost the ball. It bounced away. One of the "shirts" snagged it, turned, and started driving down the court.

"What the hell happened to you, Hitchcock?" the coach yelled.

My fellow "skins" glared at me.

"Hamstring," I said, reaching down to hold

my leg. I limped off the court and sat on the bleachers.

I was back. Somehow I must have finally fallen asleep in Everworld. Hard to imagine. I'd been lying there on clean straw beside dirty men, staring up into blank darkness and trying to think about anything, anything besides that pyramid.

But I had fallen asleep. It was the only way I could possibly be here. Back in the real world. It's the way it worked. We didn't know why. Fall asleep in Everworld, you woke up back in the old life, the old body, with two intact sets of memories: the dull, ordinary details of another dull, ordinary day of school and home and more school. And you had the memories of the other side. Memories that were not so dull.

It, like the real me, the normal me, the me that didn't attack Aztec gods with Viking swords, got a little update every now and then. And vice versa. Like I, we, both of me were tuning in to CNN every once in a while and learning about what was going on with the other self.

Oh, interesting, I see I got a B-plus on the chem test.

Oh, interesting, I see I'm about to have my heart ripped out to feed Big H.

Well, thanks for the update. Good luck getting to third base on your date Saturday!

Thanks, and good luck to you in escaping from cannibal hell. See ya!

The others. I had to find the others. But there was still another ten minutes before we were supposed to hit the showers.

Somehow, somehow, I didn't know how, we had to stay here. We had to not go back.

Maybe there was some copy of me over there, too bad. As long as I, Christopher, the brain, the memories, the thoughts, the sense of humor, the nasty, self-interested creature called Christopher, isn't there, I don't care. Huitzilopoctli can eat my heart. As long as I'm not there to see it.

"Coach!" I yelled too loudly.

"What do you want, Hitchcock?"

"I need to see the nurse. Need a couple aspirin or whatever before this swells up."

"Uh-huh. You are the laziest human being I've ever met."

"Can I go?"

"You're no good to anyone here," he said.

I took off, careful to hobble as I went. Once in the locker room I showered fast, slipped on my clothes, and went looking for David.

Instead, I found April. She was in the hall, heading for the library.

"Oh, man!" I yelled.

She nodded, cautious. Amused, too.

I grabbed her arm and pulled her aside, practically shoving her into a locker.

"Where are you?" I hissed.

"Um, right here?" She pried my fingers loose.

"No, I mean on the other side. Where are you in Everworld?"

She shrugged. "Last I knew we were still on the longboat, heading for an attack on the Aztecs."

"You haven't fallen asleep yet," I said. "Either that, or . . . or I don't know," I finished lamely.

"How'd it go?" April asked.

"What?"

"The battle."

"We didn't exactly win," I said, trying to keep my instinct for sarcasm under control.

"Is anyone hurt?"

"Of us, no. Not yet. Although you, maybe, we don't know where you are. Sven's dead. Olaf's dead. And the rest of us are being held, pending the removal of our freaking hearts, after which we will be barbecued and served up buffet-style with coleslaw and baked beans!"

I had failed to control my sarcasm. I was nearly screaming. I was spitting on her with each percussive sound.

"Where am I?" April demanded, scared.

"We don't know. But you were back with the boats which, trust me, all belong to Huitzilo-poctli's happy crew now."

Her face was pale. The huge green eyes grew more huge.

"Oh, my God. They could be . . . I could be . . ."

"Entertaining the Aztec warriors? Yeah."

She looked sick. That had been a harsh thing for me to say. I do that when I'm scared. I take cheap shots at people. Not one of my more attractive personality traits.

"What if I've been killed?" she asked. She put her hand on my arm.

She's a babe. Any other time I'd be doing a nice tingle and thinking, *My backseat or yours?* But I knew better. This wasn't a romantic touch. This was a "tell me it's all going to be okay" touch. I couldn't tell her it was okay. It wasn't.

I said, "Not to sound cold, April, but if you're dead over there, cool. That means we can survive dying over there. Believe me, with what's happening to me over there, I'd love to find out death isn't fatal."

She nodded. Slowly. Still looking sick. "And if

it is fatal? I could, what, drop dead any second because of something that's happening to me in Everworld? Something I don't even know about?"

"Have you seen David or Jalil?"

It took her a few seconds to respond. She was far away. I thought for a minute she'd snapped back. You know, that the Everworld April had arrived. But then, no.

"I saw Jalil in class. Just now. He didn't give me a look or anything. Are you sure both of them are alive?"

"Last I checked. I think I'd have woken up if someone came along to drag them away."

"What do we do?" she asked.

"Oh, gee, I don't know, I guess we go to our next class and wait to see if . . . I don't know. I don't know! This is bizarre. How do you make sense of this? How do you figure your life out when you're late for a class *and* about to be sacrificed to a pagan deity? I don't know which life to lead. Any second now I could wake up and boom, I'm back there, and then I, the me who's left here, I go around like you're going around now. Waiting to find out what happens when they cut the heart out of Everworld Christopher."

That vise was around my chest again, tightening, tightening.

"I wish I would go to sleep," April said. "Then at least I'd know where I was."

A teacher passed by right about then. She must have overheard part of what April said. The teacher shook her head slightly and walked on.

"We keep this up, pretty soon we'll be dead over there and in a looney bin here," I said.

"We need to find David," April said.

"What's he going to do?"

"I don't know. Something. I hope."

I was kind of hurt. April had just dissed me without meaning to. David would do something. Me? What was I good for? Not much, I guess.

The bell rang. Doors all down the hallway flew open. Kids exploded out of their classrooms, yelling and talking and laughing and running and swinging their backpacks up onto their shoulders.

David appeared. Jalil was with him.

"Are you here or there?" I snapped.

"I'm asleep," Jalil answered. "David's not."

"Come on, let's get out of here," I said.

"I can't cut last period!" April protested.

Suddenly, I was back in a dark room full of smelly men. "No!" I yelled.

Jalil jerked awake. David? Gone. Not in sight.

I looked around, trying to see what had awak-

ened me. There were Aztec warriors making their
way through the flopped-out throng.

A half-dozen heavily armed warriors. And two
characters who looked like Pig Pen from Peanuts.
All grown up, and still refusing to bathe.

They wore black. Probably. It was hard to tell
what color their long robes might have once
been. Their hair was long, matted, sticking out in
dreadlocks, hanging in greasy strands.

Their faces were blackened. Not black black,
because unlike the Vikings, who had evidently
welcomed all races to their happy little Looney
Tunes world, the Aztecs were all identically copper-
skinned and black-haired. These guys were black
not from melanin but from soot and cinders and
a complete aversion to soap.

I'd only thought the Vikings smelled. The
Vikings were walking, talking Clinique sales-
people compared to these two. The Vikings were
dirty by accident. These two had made a career
out of being filthy.

The reek was intense, powerful, hideous, and
disturbing. It was the reek of body odor and dirt
and fungus. But most of all, it was the stench of
dried blood.

The two walking sewers, and their escort of
well-groomed warriors, picked their way gingerly
through the snoring bodies.

From time to time they would point at one of the Vikings. Then the guards would rouse the Norseman, not unkindly, and pass him along, unescorted, to the far end of the room.

"Priests," Jalil commented.

"What are they doing?"

He slid his eyes sideways to look at me. "Choosing up teams for the big volleyball tournament. How would I know what they're doing? I'm as ignorant as you. Almost. But if I was to guess, I'd say they're ordering off the menu."

The priests kept coming. Should we sidle away? Or would that draw attention? It was like some awful version of the old classroom game: Keep the teacher from calling on you.

Jalil and I pretended to go back to sleep.

Breathe, Christopher, I told myself.

"These two," the priest said. "Young. Their hearts will be tender and unblemished."

CHAPTER IX

I could have said, "No! Not me!" I didn't.

I stood up. Shaky. Numb. Like I couldn't quite feel my own body. Maybe I was trying to convince myself I wasn't really here. Maybe I wanted to believe that I was back there, back in the world, back in school, in a familiar hallway, standing by lockers, talking to my friends, far away, not here.

It couldn't be real. Could not be.

I stumbled, a step behind Jalil. The warriors were almost gentle in their treatment. Respectful, even. Not just to us but to the Vikings as well.

The Vikings went along like sheep. We did, too. But I guess I expected more from the Norsemen. They just hung their heads and shuffled along.

"Where's David?" I asked Jalil.

He shook his head.

"Figures he would find a way to hide out," I said bitterly.

We were outside. The moon cast a blue glow over the city. Golden adobe walls and terra-cotta roofs and volcanic black cobblestones were all blue and silver, shadows and darkness.

The air was humid. Jungle air. Warm, even at night. Thick. But there were no mosquitoes. Strange. Maybe Huitzilopoctli had banished them. Maybe he didn't want any competition for the blood supply.

I did see rats, or something awfully much like rats, scurrying across our path, trundling along the bases of walls.

They marched us along the street in near silence but for the shuffle of feet. Maybe two, maybe three hundred of us, guarded by no more than twenty warriors.

"Not many guards," I whispered to Jalil.

He nodded. "They're armed, we're not. But it's not like they're carrying shotguns or machine guns. One guy with a stone sword can't stop ten times his own number."

It was weird. We could have taken the guards down. We didn't. No one but us even seemed to be thinking about it. The guards themselves were laid-back. Relaxed.

"Come on," I said. "No one said we have to keep up." I jerked my head subtly.

Jalil caught my hint. We started walking a little more slowly, letting the Vikings flow around us. Maybe I was looking for David. Maybe I was just looking for an opportunity. Something. Anything.

What we found was Thorolf. He's a picture-book Viking: big, big arms, big chest, big beard. An older guy. Middle-aged. Not a kid. But we liked him. Thorolf was about as close as you could get to a mellow Viking.

"Thorolf!" I whispered.

"Yes, it is me. More the shame."

He didn't look like himself. Not the bluff, loud, backslapping, guffawing guy we knew.

Then again, I wasn't exactly myself, either. Imminent death will do that to you.

"Thorolf, we can take these guys," I whispered. "There's hundreds of us. Just a handful of them."

He looked puzzled. "We are prisoners."

"What Christopher is suggesting is, maybe we don't have to stay prisoners," Jalil said.

Thorolf kept on looking dumb. "We lost the battle. Their power was greater than ours."

"Yeah, we were there, dude," I said. "We know who lost and who won. But that was before. Right now we outnumber these guys about ten or fif-

teen to one. Bada-bing, bada-boom, we take them
down, run for the gate, make it to the boats, and
haul butt."

"Their god is too powerful. Even Mjolnir
wielded by Olaf Ironfoot could not defeat him."

"Maybe Big H — Huitzilopoctli, I mean —
maybe he's asleep. I mean, it's night, right?"

Jalil jumped in with his usual "I've figured it all
out" tone of voice. "If there are still warriors in
this society it can only mean that Huitzilopoctli
limits his involvement. I mean, why would those
guys still be training and practicing and making
weapons and so on, if all they had to do was dial
up Big H every time they ran into trouble?"

"What he said," I urged Thorolf, pointing at
Jalil. "Come on, man. Give the word. Let's take
these guys out!"

"Give it up."

David! He was just a few paces behind us.

"Oh, so nice of you to join us," I said, torn between relief and annoyance.

He shrugged. "I didn't go anywhere. I've spent
the night trying to get some of these guys to work
on an escape. No luck. Not happening."

We sidled back from Thorolf to join David.

"They don't get it," David explained. "For
these guys the battle was it. The last word. They
bring Mjolnir, the Aztecs bring Big H, everyone's

brave and heroic, our side loses. So that's it. Now they're prisoners. The end."

Jalil nodded. "I was afraid that was it. Fatalism."

"Fatal is right," I muttered.

"It's a fatalistic outlook," Jalil went on, probably soothed by the sound of his own brain churning. "It's what comes of believing that great supernatural powers control your life."

"Yeah, well, great supernatural powers do," I said. "Or didn't you happen to notice the big blue guy with the snake on his arm?"

"No. Bull. I'm not saying Huitzilopoctli isn't real. I'm just saying he doesn't seem to be able to keep his people fed. And anyway, Olaf knocked Big H's arm off with Mjolnir. So he's not invulnerable."

We had reached the end of our march. We had gone around what looked like the back side of the pyramid. There was a large building there, four stories tall, with no windows and a single large door. The door was open, a rectangle of golden, welcoming light.

The head of our column started through.

"Now or maybe never," David said.

"The three of us, alone?" Jalil said. He shook his head. "You ask me to commit suicide before I can be murdered? Uh-uh. There may still come a better chance."

I hesitated, waffling between the two of them. Then, I heard a strange, incongruous sound. The sound of a female voice giggling.

"There may be a better chance," I said.

We reached the doorway. Stepped through, behind the first hundred or so Vikings.

Inside there was a line of nine priests. A Supreme Court of dirt, crusted blood, and odor. Several of them had knotted cords of thorns passed through their tongues, lips, cheeks, ears. Some of the thorns were an inch long. There were lacerations from pushing the thorns through the flesh. Sideways, in some cases. Some of the priests had ears that looked like the fringe on a buckskin jacket.

The Aztec priests took their body piercing very seriously.

At one end of the room was the best buffet table I'd ever seen. Huge mounds of bananas, mangoes, brilliantly red tomatoes, and something that looked like cactus with the prickles removed. It was like the exotic produce section of the supermarket, times ten. There was roasted corn and roasted potatoes. Eggs in a dozen different sizes. Whole pigs. Whole . . . some other animal. There were pottery jars full of beverages. Flowers. Pastries. Tortillas. Beans.

It was a brunch at the Aztec Hyatt Regency.

But, as hungry as I suddenly was, the food was only the second most interesting thing about the room.

Because behind the line of priests were women. Young, attractive women. A lot of women. At least one, maybe two for each prisoner. A lot of pretty, underfed women, most as skinny as Courtney Cox, many with faces painted yellow, and very little clothing between them.

"Our farewell party," Jalil said mordantly.

He was right, of course. The Vikings had mentioned this aspect of Aztec behavior. For the Aztecs, feeding your heart to Huitzilopoctli was an honor. (One they themselves tried hard to avoid.) They figured the human sacrifices should be in good shape, well-fed, and happy. They were going to stuff us full of food and booze they themselves didn't have enough of. All to make us fit for Huitzilopoctli.

The Aztecs were giving us a nice send-off. But still, a send-off.

And yet, I thought, *if you gotta have your heart ripped out, you might as well enjoy the last few hours.*

CHAPTER
X

"Eat up," David said. "But stay away from the women."

"Yeah? How about, forget you?" I said. I grabbed a fried plantain and a piece of what was probably ham. Maybe ham. There were two attractive women draped around me, clinging, hands reaching here and there with very pleasurable effect. "Did someone die and make you God, David? Must have missed that."

"Is that ham any good?" Jalil asked.

I took a big, ripping bite and chewed it in David's face. "Yeah, it's very tasty. Wish I had some yams to go with it."

Jalil nodded. "That young lady on your arm there? That's what she'll be saying about you: tasty. Wish she had some yams to go with you."

Jalil was right. Later, tomorrow or whenever,

this skinny girl would be gorging herself sick on my left calf, ripping at it with her tiny white teeth, smacking her lips, enjoying the crispy, crunchy, fire-roasted skin. . . .

"Get away," I muttered. I gave her a shove. Not a harsh shove. Not as harsh as I ought to give someone who was thinking of whether she'd have me broiled or fried.

She shrugged and took her friend off with her.

The Vikings, needless to say, were not even slightly restrained. All around us was a TV evangelist's vision of hell: gluttony, drunkenness, and more different types of wanton behavior than you see on Cinemax late at night.

My vision of heaven. If you left out the part where they cut out your heart and eat you.

"You know what?" David whispered to Jalil and me as we huddled together like the three biggest losers ever to blow a cool party.

"What?" I moaned, unable to stop myself from looking around at everything I was missing.

"I don't know if anyone has ever tried to escape from the Aztecs, but I know one thing for sure: If anyone ever did try, they didn't try during this particular phase."

Jalil nodded. Even he looked wistful. "Guess not, probably. Most are like Thorolf. They figure it's fate."

"So we book?" I said skeptically.

"Yeah," David said, putting on his crud-eating, fear-nothing, James Bond grin.

Save me from insecure jerks with hero fixations. I looked at Jalil. Jalil was a prickly, self-serving know-it-all, but he wasn't trying to prove to the world that he was Conan the Barbarian.

"Now or maybe never," Jalil said.

He looked sick. I nodded in approval. I trust a guy who looks sick when he's getting ready to do something suicidal. If I'd had a mirror I'd have seen one sick face looking back at me. Ninety percent of the trouble in this world comes from guys who think they have something to prove.

"You know what we do?" I suggested. "We walk right out the door."

David nodded. "Yeah. Like we're going outside for a smoke or to take a leak."

"Cool and calm," Jalil agreed. "Then, when they try and grab us, we run. But where? Which way?"

"Out of this city," I suggested. "Into the jungle."

"April," David said.

"We can't help April dead," I said harshly.

"We all go home together, or no one goes," David said. "Us, April, Senna."

"Yeah, whatever," I said.

"Not the jungle. Down the shore," Jalil said. "Down the beach, that's a footrace. Maybe we can win. But into the jungle, that's about animals and bugs and quicksand and being chased by guys who know the jungle a lot better than we do."

Made sense to me. I jerked to my feet very quickly. I didn't want to have a deal with David doing a big "Let's go, team!" thing.

I wiped my sweaty palms down my pant legs. "I would trade my mother for an Uzi," I muttered.

The three of us walked through the wild, drunken, gulping, pleasuring crowd. We looked like a trio of missionaries who'd stumbled into Caligula's New Year's Eve party.

Legs stiff-casual, arms jerking with a pathetic, overdone display of nonchalance, we headed for the door, still open to the warm night air.

Two guys made up with eagle feathers and craft-show eagle hats stood there, arms crossed over their hairless chests. Closer. Closer. My eyes strained for the first sign that the two eagle knights would whip out their obsidian swords and hack us to death.

"Laugh," David whispered tersely. "Talk."

"Ah-hah-hah-hah!" Jalil said.

"Yeah, you are so right!" David yelped with idiot enthusiasm. "The Cubbies are going all the way this time. Hah-hah-hah!"

"You're killin' me, that is so funny!" I said with the kind of phony cheer you usually reserve for visits with Great-aunt Whatever at the old folks' home.

Closer. Closer. Nothing. No movement. No reaction.

I grinned at one of the guards. "Great party!"

He reached for his sword hilt.

I swung. Big, dumb right-hand aimed straight for his chin. I missed his chin and caught him in the side of the head.

Swung again. Caught air.

The sword was out. The second guy was moving fast. David slammed into him, knocking him back against the doorjamb.

My guy whipped his sword in an uppercut that swished a millimeter from my chin. I fell. I kicked. A little of both. My foot caught shinbone.

I slammed on my back, wind gone. Jalil swung on my guy. Connected with his ear. My guy staggered. David was all over his guy, swarming him with short punches, staying in close, gasping like a beached fish.

I crawled, tried to fill my lungs, staggered up just as my guy went down. I snatched his sword from his weakened grip and took a wild swing. Obsidian flakes caught in his collarbone. I yanked the sword out.

All this with no yelling. No cries of alarm. Grunts of surprise and effort and pain.

"They don't box," David said, panting.

His victim's face was a mess from a dozen hard, short jabs. The guy hadn't even managed to draw his sword. The guy looked like his brain had been knocked into next week. Confused, stupid.

"Let's haul," Jalil said.

Into the night, running, sneakers on flagstones bouncing weird, UFO echoes off the walls. My heart was hammering. Huitzilopoctli would hear it! He would hear my heart and come to take it from me.

I still had the heavy, awkward sword.

"Which way?" David asked.

It was dark. Not civilization dark. This was no-streetlight dark. Middle-of-the-woods dark. The moon was behind the clouds. We could easily lose one another in this dark. And we had long since lost our way.

Then, not fifty feet away, we saw her.

She shone as if the moon were sending down a single, tight, floodlight beam just for her.

Senna.

CHAPTER

XI

Senna wore a long robe with a hood that was folded back to show her hair and face.

She said nothing. We stopped.

"Senna!" David cried.

She turned and began to move away. Walking quickly, almost seeming to glide.

David started after her. Jalil grabbed his arm.

"No," Jalil warned.

David shook him off. "She's trying to lead us to someplace safe."

Senna had stopped, still fifty feet away. Waiting. Silent.

"This feels bad, man," I whispered. "Why doesn't she say anything?"

"Doesn't want to wake up the whole neighborhood," David said.

Suddenly, from back in the direction we'd come from, an uproar. Loud, male voices.

"You know a way out of this city?" David demanded of Jalil and me.

I shook my head. "But I don't trust her."

"I'm going with her," David said. He started walking.

Jalil and I looked at each other. All either of us saw was the whites of wide-scared eyes.

"This is bull," I said.

"Yeah," he agreed. "But we have to stick together."

"She's the cause of all this," I argued. But already I was in lockstep with Jalil, following David, following Senna, feeling like, *Oh, God, it's just getting worse, and I wouldn't have thought that was possible.*

The uproar of angry voices grew louder behind us. I quickened my pace. Senna. Senna would show us the way out. *Yeah,* I told myself, *sure, yeah, she'd get us out of this.* Senna was our friend. Senna was one of us, freaky, yeah, but one of us, from the real world. I'd made out with her, after all, we'd been close, I'd gotten to second base, that had to count for something.

So why was she shining like a dashboard saint? Why was she silent? Why did she keep her distance?

Down a darker than dark street, she led us, led us with her own eerie light. Led us on with a feeling of dread that mixed with hope and left the dread all the stronger.

I so wanted to be home.

A turn. Down an alley. David stopped. We caught up with him. The three of us stared down that alley. Nothing. No Senna. No way out. Dead end.

"There must be a way out," David said. "She went somewhere. A doorway. We have to find it."

A rush of sandaled feet on stone. I spun around. A dozen warriors. More coming. The escape was over.

"She wants us dead, man," Jalil said. "She wants us dead."

Hard to argue with that. Because we were sure dead now.

CHAPTER XII

The first time I really noticed Senna was at a pool party at her house. Not Senna's party, of course — she'd never do anything so normal.

It was April's party. April and Senna are half sisters. Hard to believe they share any DNA at all.

April has all the charm, all the flirty smiles and the knowing winks and the deep, rich laughs. April is like her name: she's springtime. You're around her, you start feeling that maybe life is okay, maybe there's nothing to worry about, maybe you'll get into the great school and get the great job and marry someone like April and still party with your friends when you're thirty years old.

Not that she's even slightly airheaded or giggly, it's not like that. It's just that April makes you think she's been out the door, had a good long look at life, and decided it's safe. She's not idiot-happy. She's wise-happy.

Senna would not be like that. It's not that she's depressed like some whiny chick singer with an acoustic guitar. Depressed is boring. Senna is not boring.

Senna is the night to her half sister's day. She's that night where you're wide-awake and the energy inside you is making you drum your fingers and hitch your shoulders and bounce your leg impatiently. Senna's the night you cruise the streets, driving slow, eyes so alert, so hungry for something, something dangerous and sexy.

Senna's a magician, always promising to reveal, always hiding what's important. Confusing, obscuring, misleading.

Walk along this dark alley with me, Christopher. Why? I won't say. I'll only smile. And when you ask whether there's anything to fear, I'll say, "Yes, Christopher. Wasn't that what you wanted?"

She'd been at school, of course. But it's a big school. Lots of girls. I hadn't noticed her. Why? I have a theory. I think I didn't notice Senna because Senna didn't want to be noticed. Not by me. Not yet.

But at that party, April's pool party, Senna had wanted me to see her, to focus on her, for my mouth to go dry, for my arms and legs to feel weak.

Strange, freaky girl. Never underestimate the dark side of the Force.

I'd always been the one in charge in previous relationships. I'm a big, glib, smart guy. I'm an expert at holding people at arm's length, at using wit to manipulate the distance between us.

I wasn't in charge with Senna.

She walked around the pool, one of those wrap-around skirts drifting open, a drink in one hand, the other hand resting just below her navel, a thumb hooked in the waist of her skirt, like a guy would hook a thumb in his jeans.

I made some dumb joke through the cotton in my mouth. She made a smile. I asked her if I could have a sip of her drink. She said no. I asked if she was there alone. She looked at me. Appraising. Serious. "I don't know," she said.

Stupid, the things you remember sometimes, huh? Stupid, the things that can fire up your imagination. A thumb in a waist, a refusal. A look that challenged me and made me realize instantly that I would fail the challenge.

Senna.

I never loved her; I knew, from that first moment I knew she'd betray me. But, good lord, I had wanted her.

As for her? I'm not as dumb as I may act sometimes. I knew she had no real interest in me, as me. You know? I knew she was looking down at me the whole time, not impressed. Not reached. Not touched. Not by me. Not really.

See, I knew she was using me for something, setting me up, making plans for me, me as a pawn, me as a tool, me as something she could pick up or put down as she chose.

Here's the sick thing? When she stopped seeing me I was a wreck. Not because I'd ever thought she would love me or sleep with me or be mine, all mine.

I was crushed because I'd felt her closing in, the predator to my prey. And I wanted her to destroy me. I guess I felt like in that moment of destruction, I would really know her. Understand something.

Now she had destroyed me. And still I knew nothing.

CHAPTER XIII

No Aztec love party this time. No food. No babes. A locked room. A toilet, no bath. A big, thick wooden door and stone walls and guards outside. The three of us sitting on our butts on stone, knees on elbows.

Maybe no one had ever tried to escape from the Aztecs before. That didn't mean they couldn't adjust.

"Had to be a mistake," David kept muttering. "She didn't lead us down there to trap us."

"You know, this faith you have in Senna is really romantic and touching and all, but you're a damned idiot!" I raged after about his tenth time. "She leads us all into this lunatic asylum to begin with, and next time we see her it's to lead us down a blind alley. So how about you get your head out of your butt, David? 'Cause here's a clue: She's not Snow Freaking White, and you aren't Prince Charming."

"Not the next time," David said.

Jalil sighed. "What?"

"I've seen her before this. After the lake, before this."

That got my attention. "Say what?"

"I saw her on the other side. In the bookstore. At least, it was, I don't know, like a vision."

"Your fantasies are not really all that relevant," Jalil said dismissively.

"It wasn't a fantasy. She was there. She told me there was going to be a big battle. Told me to stay out of it."

I swear if I'd had that sword back I'd have laid it into the dumb jerk's head.

"Heard her again, in my head," David said, staring down at the floor. "When the battle started. She said 'Run away. Run away, David.' She's not trying to kill us. She wants to save us."

"Hey, David. You're a Jew, right?"

"Half Jewish," he said.

"Yeah? Well you know the word 'schmuck'? Did I pronounce that right? 'Schmuck'? Or maybe you'd prefer a good old-fashioned Anglo-Saxon word, you —"

"Back off," David warned.

"Back off?" I yelled. "Back off? You hold out on us, you lead us after that evil chick, down that alley, so now here we are, trapped again, waiting to die —" My voice broke.

I put my head in my hands. I wanted to cry. I guess I did. How could I be there? How could I be there, waiting to die?

"I want to sleep, man," I said.

"That'd be good," David said. "Cross over, maybe get in touch with April. Find out where she is, how she's doing."

"We may not want to know," Jalil said.

"Can't sleep anyway, man," I said. "Can't sleep. In a couple hours . . . What are we going to do?"

"Had to be a mistake," David mumbled into his hands. "Senna didn't set us up. Had to be a mistake. We were too slow. She didn't have enough time. Probably our own fault."

David muttered about Senna. Jalil sat there talking to himself, spinning theories about Everworld, trying to figure out logically whether dying here meant death in the real world, or whether death here would merely bring us freedom from this awful place.

For a while I made responsive grunts to Jalil.

Then I stopped listening. David had his delusion. Jalil had his. David's world was somehow going to be about him playing hero. Jalil's world was going to somehow, somehow make sense. He was trying to keep his little house of logic Legos standing.

Me, I had no delusion. I just wanted to live. I just wanted to go home. What I had instead was imagination. Terrible thing, imagination is. See, without imagination you can't picture every horrible detail in advance. Without imagination death is just death. With imagination, death is detailed. Detailed and specific and so real.

No one slept. Hours dragged. Hurry up, get it over with. Hurry up and die.

Turn off my brain! Turn off the feeling, the so-terribly-real feeling of being grabbed by strong hands and bent back, back over the altar, the sight of filthy priestly faces intent on their work, as indifferent to me as a butcher is to a hog.

Obsidian knife rising.

Stomach muscles screaming.

Heart beating, oh, beating, beating, the bare skin of my chest vibrating with each desperate rhythm.

Feeling the jagged-edged knife cut.

Seeing the hands, the filthy, blood-caked hands diving into my own chest . . .

No.

No.

The door opened. Brilliant sunlight made me squint, made me cover my eyes.

No.

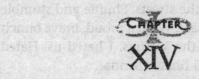

CHAPTER XIV

The three of us stumbled outside. Out into clean, pure sunlight, still low on the horizon.

The Vikings were being assembled in the street. Hungover. Hair twisted. Beards matted. Dried vomit on their clothes. Exotic fruits and legs of lamb stuck in their belts and pockets, you know, in case they got hungry waiting to be eviscerated, in case the wait to die worked up an appetite.

I spotted Thorolf. As much a wreck as the rest. Eyes blinking owlishly. Expression resigned, defeated.

The other Vikings I'd known by name were gone. Sven Swordeater. Olaf Ironfoot.

"I don't see April," Jalil said.

"Maybe she's okay," David said. "She was with the boats. Maybe she's okay."

"Or dead," I grated.

The guards started us all moving. There were more guards today. I guess our example made them nervous.

We shuffled along, foot after foot, making a noise like some gigantic sack of dirt being dragged through the streets. Shuffle and stumble and mutter and glare. What a proud, brave bunch we were. I hated the Vikings. I hated us. Hated myself. Most of all I hated Senna.

So bright. So sunny. Bad things didn't happen on sunny days.

Down the street. Onto the vast, open plaza. They waited there, silent, impossibly silent, a thousand, ten, hundreds of thousands! Thin, gaunt, staring black eyes in deep sunken sockets, staring at us as we stumbled past. Staring at us. Staring at the food some of the Vikings carried.

All of New Tenochtitlan was turned out around the base of the pyramid, back at a safe distance, standing clear, holding in neat lines in neat rectangles, men, women, silent children. All bright and dark at once.

Soldiers, better-fed, taller, stronger, arrogant in ludicrous feathers and animal hats, were in front in a single file that outlined the masses.

We stopped. Like train commuters who'd reached a turnstile, we milled in disorder. Up ahead, not far enough ahead, too close, the priests were shoving the beaten men into a double line. Two by two, up the steps.

The pyramid was steps on steps. The basic construction, the blocks themselves, formed narrow, steep steps. But a broader, gentler stairway had been layered over this, still steep, but not so anyone would be likely to fall. To our left a central stairway of sorts, for more-than-human feet and legs. I could have climbed those stairs, too, but it would have been more climbing than walking.

Ahead of the three of us I saw the first rank of Vikings climbing. Up they went, the head of the snake that extended up out of the mass of victims.

They climbed, and the priests shoved, and suddenly it was my turn, suddenly filthy hands grabbed by biceps and shoved me into place, like an impatient first-grade teacher lining up the kids for a fire drill.

Jalil was beside me. David behind.

First step. Oh, God, we were climbing. Oh, God.

No.

Lift foot. Put foot down. Thigh and calf muscles work. Lift foot. Put foot down.

Oh, God. I was climbing. Had to stop. Had to stop! Had to stop!

Lift foot. Put foot down. Thigh and calf muscles work.

Legs shaking, quivering from the effort. Stomach wanting to heave. Heart . . . heart . . .

No!

Lift foot. Put foot down. Thigh and calf muscles.

I squinted to look ahead. Sunlight blinding. So far above us, but already too close. The head of the line was reaching the top. The black-robed priests waited.

We'd just go back over, that was it, Jalil was right, we'd die here, but we'd be back over there, laughing about it all, wondering if it was all just a dream, laughing, all of us together going, "Man, was that weird or what?"

I tripped.

David, behind me, put a hand out to steady me. Thanks. Thanks, David, wouldn't want a bruise, wouldn't want to fall and hurt myself. Oh, God, we were climbing.

The line stopped.

Then he appeared. Huitzilopoctli.

Huitzilopoctli stepped out of his temple and stood there, legs spread wide, towering over the dozens of priests.

"His arm," Jalil croaked. "Didn't heal. Still gone. He has limits. He can be hurt."

I snorted in absolute contempt. Jalil still believed he was going to think his way out of this. Was he out of his stupid, stupid mind? Didn't he see?

He looked at me. Our eyes locked. Yeah, he saw. He knew he was just making noise to drive away the panic. He knew.

Four priests came hustling out from offstage. They carried a turquoise pillow, holding it up for their evil god like they were offering him a mint. From that angle I couldn't see what was on the pillow, but then Huitzilopoctli reached down and raised a tiny, toylike Mjolnir.

It looked ridiculous in his massive hand. And I guess he thought so, too, because he held it up, displayed it for all to see,

Silence.

Then, Huitzilopoctli laughed.

And everyone in the plaza below us laughed, too. I had forgotten them. But hearing that echo of laughter I twisted my head around and saw the spreading crowd. They seemed so far down.

The effect on the Vikings was what you'd expect. Mjolnir was as much magic as they had. And now it was Huitzilopoctli's toy. They'd flashed the cross at a vampire and had the vampire laugh.

Then, having milked the desperate, near-hysterical laughs, Huitzilopoctli lay Mjolnir back down on the pillow. The priests hustled Mjolnir away, and the blood-mad god stepped back into his temple.

The line began to move.

I couldn't see the first killing. Or the next or the next. They were cut off from sight by the heads of those before me and the angle of the steps.

I couldn't see the first forty or sixty or a hundred killings. But at that point I began to see the stream. The sludgy, slow-moving stream of red that trickled and poured and congealed its horrifying way down the steps to our left.

It was blood over blood. The wet and fresh over the baked and crusted. The higher we climbed, the thicker the crust. The higher we climbed, the quicker the stream.

And then came the bodies. They rolled down. Stopped. Were kicked and shoved by lines of sweating priests.

Bodies untouched, except that in each there gaped a black-red wound, a hole where a heart had been.

Lift foot. Put foot down. Thigh and calf muscles.

Stop! Stop! Stop!

Lift foot. Put foot down.

Why couldn't I stop? Stop! Run! Run away!

Lift foot . . .

So close now. A sound. Oh, no, no, no, no. The sound of knife in flesh. The grunt of pain. The grunt of effort. The sound of wet scooping . . .

A line of women arrayed up the steps. A dozen. Hoods, cloaks, faces half-shaded.

Not looking at us, we were dead! No . . . one looking. Looking hard. Green eyes. Red hair.

April!

A dozen steps above us. She moved her head so slightly, side to side. "No," she signaled. Quiet.

Quiet? Why? To save her? To keep her from being found out? Screw her! No, no, no, Christopher, die a man, die a man. Help her live. Be a man.

I nudged Jalil. I met his eyes then carried his gaze over to her.

I twisted back to see David. He'd already spotted her.

The sound of blade on meat.

The ripple of blood trickling slowly in the heat.

The smell of it.

I looked at April. Silent, she mouthed a single word.

"Mjolnir."

CHAPTER
XVI

"What?" Jalil whispered to me.

"The hammer," I said.

April was just ahead now, we were almost abreast of her. Her robe parted ever so slightly. I saw pale flesh.

I saw steel.

"You up for this?" David asked softly.

Up for it? I was shaking in every muscle. I was drenched in my own fear sweat. I was ten minutes from having my heart cut out and fed to a creature that couldn't possibly exist.

"I like it better than the alternative," I managed to say.

"On three. One."

Lift foot.

"Two."

Put foot down.

"Three!"

I jerked my quivering muscles, broke from the line, and went for April like she was a lifeline and I was a drowning man.

Robe open!

Sword! Ax! A long knife! Viking weapons. Steel!

Hands fumbling, grabbing, missing, heart, gasping, heart, had it! My hand closed on the haft of an ax with a two-foot handle, a curved blade on one side and a pickax on the other.

"Go for the top!" David yelled, and I didn't need encouragement. The four of us plowed through and around the Viking line, onto the blood-slicked steps, running, leaping, scraping knees, climbing, up and running, running across the platform, the foul, reeking platform.

A Viking stretched out on the black altar, priest on his hands, priest holding his legs, knife high in the air, poised over a bared, blond-haired chest. Thorolf.

The knife man gaped, outraged, like I'd just farted in church and giggled about it. I ran straight at him. He was still gaping when I swung that ax. His head kept the expression as it rolled down the steps.

No soldiers! Priests, black, filth-encrusted, their flesh mortified by thorns. They ran, confused, then came rushing back.

"Damn it, Thorolf, get up!" I yelled.

I swung my ax at the line of priests. Jalil and David jabbed at them. What a surprise: The priests were not exactly profiles in courage.

They backed up again, yelling, praying, screaming, mad and scared and worried that things had gone suddenly strange at their little picnic.

"The hammer, you idiots!" April yelled. "Get the stupid hammer before he comes!"

I saw the hammer. Still on its cushion, atop a platform like an auxiliary, backup altar. I knew who April meant by "he."

The temple was impossibly tall above us. Open, yet dark. He could be just inside, watching, laughing, ready to come for us, ready to take over for his priests and murder us himself.

I jolted toward the hammer. David sword-whipped a warrior who'd come rushing up.

A sudden blow. I was down, breathless! What?

A priest had plowed into me. I jumped up, kicked him, leaped over, and ran, racing Jalil for the hammer.

The mass of priests charged at last. Too late!

The cushion. The hammer.

My fingers closed around the stunted handle of Thor's hammer.

The priests stopped. Stared. Babbled to one another in renewed confusion. That was okay, because the four of us were pretty lost, too.

"The Vikings," Jalil gasped, winded. "Show them the hammer."

I raced back to the edge of the platform. I held that hammer up in the air over my head. I yelled at the top of my lungs, "Mjolnir! The hammer of Thor! Come on, you bunch of babies, let's kick some Aztec butt!"

An excellent speech. A real cinematic moment.

Only I realized that the Vikings were no longer looking at me. They were looking behind me.

I felt the flesh on my back creep.

Slowly turned my head, slowly my eyes, all in slow motion, molasses. Towering over me. His one remaining hand clutched a dripping red mass. Red stained his mouth and chin.

I spun, kicked my leg out, whipped around, and like a pro pitcher throwing out a runner, I let fly with Mjolnir.

The hammer flew.

Huitzilopoctli just had time to look down before Thor's sledge hit him in the feathery loincloth.

The hammer came sailing back toward me, but I was too gone to notice. It sailed past.

Huitzilopoctli grunted. He got a "now I'm going to kill you!" look on his blue-and-gold face.

Then, slowly, slowly, he crumpled. Like a guy who's standing on his bike pedals when the chain breaks, he crumpled.

"Look out! He'll crush us!" April yelled. She jerked me aside.

David and Jalil ran. I ran. April ran.

Huitzilopoctli yelled out in agony.

He fell.

The Vikings roared to life.

The Aztecs moaned.

We were over that platform, around the side of the temple, and heading down the far side by the time we heard Big H hit the steps.

"April?" I gasped.

"Yeah?"

"I am your slave for life."

Chapter
XVII

No sleep, coming off battle, coming off an aborted escape, coming off that awful march up the side of that hideous pyramid. We were exhausted. Beyond exhaustion.

We wandered, lost in the streets of the city of Huitzilopoctli for an hour before we located a gate.

An hour during which time the sounds of combat and pillage and depredation grew louder, then fainter, then louder again.

Mjolnir had woken the Vikings out of their slumber. They had no swords or axes, but a thousand or more Vikings in the middle of a city is serious trouble anywhere. And they had Mjolnir. The breeze carried that cry to our ears.

"Mjolnir! Mjolnir!"

The Vikings historically didn't draw sharp

lines between killing soldiers and killing innocent civilians. I didn't care. Anyone who wanted to eat me wasn't innocent.

I ran. We ran, footsore and exhausted. Out of the gate. Out of that evil, evil city.

"The beach," Jalil said. "Still our best bet. The Aztecs will be busy with the Vikings now. We don't need anacondas and jaguars."

No one argued. We ran right back the way we'd come, away down across the battlefield. All the dead and wounded had been removed. I considered the ham I'd eaten the night before.

No, don't think about that, Christopher. You're alive, so shut up.

Onto sand. The sea. The Viking longboats were charred, smoking hulks. Charcoal boats. The Aztecs had burned them. Everything stank of drowned fires.

David cursed. "That's a crime."

"That's a crime? They burn some boats, that's what you object to in their behavior?"

"What it is is stupid," Jalil said. "All that wood. Even if they didn't know how to sail the boats, they could have salvaged the wood,"

"Let's keep moving," April pressed.

We kept moving along the beach, down the longboat graveyard.

"Nice robe," I said.

April gave me a weary smile. "What, this old thing? Just something I threw on. And now I think I'll just throw it off."

She whipped the robe off, twirled it into a ball, and threw it into a smoking hull. It began to smolder.

April still had her backpack with most of our worldly possessions. A CD player and some mostly bad music; a bottle of Advil; a book or two.

"So, what's your story?" David asked her.

"Well, I was in the boat. Saw the Vikings all come running when Huitzilopoctli showed up. I hid, but it didn't work. They found me. I thought they were going to kill me."

"Kind of was afraid they had," I admitted. "Or else . . . never mind."

"Yeah, or else," April said darkly. "I think that was the plan. Only this priest showed up. He asked me if I was a virgin."

"So naturally you lied?" I suggested.

"I said, 'Absolutely. I'm even a vegetarian.'"

I laughed. The first laugh in what felt like a million years. David and Jalil smiled.

"Anyway." April shrugged. "The priest decided I'd look good in the temple. They don't get many green-eyed redheads. So I was an official temple virgin."

"Good gig."

"Uh-huh. Till the ceremony's over. Then I think the virgins become property of the priests, who have their fun and kill the girls in another sacrifice. That's what I understood, anyway."

"Sick, messed-up people," David said. "Nazis without the tanks."

Jalil was walking backward. "I don't see anyone following us."

"They're busy," David said. "The Vikings finally got it together. I guess the hammer did it."

"Where are we going?" I wondered.

"Away from that place back there," April spat. "I just hope she makes it out of there."

We all stopped dead. "She? Who?" Jalil snapped.

April looked surprised. "Senna." She must have noticed our spooked expressions. "Yeah, I saw her. She showed me where to find the weapons I smuggled to you."

"Ha!" David yelled. "She was trying to help us."

I wasn't convinced. I knew what I'd seen. Or at least, I thought I did. But I kept my mouth shut.

"We can't leave her back there," David said flatly.

"We have no choice," Jalil said.

April said nothing. She was not rushing to the rescue of her half sister.

"We can wait till it's calmed down a little, till the heat is off us. We can go back. Find her." David nodded vigorously, trying to convince himself.

"You know what, David? On my big list of things that ain't happening, going back into New Whatever is number one. It's higher than 'sticking needles in my own eyes.' Not happening."

"She saved our lives," David argued. He stepped closer, bristling, playing the tough guy. "You're going to leave one of our own behind?"

I laughed. "David, I've just thrown down with Huitzilopoctli. You think you scare me?"

"You're just scared, period."

"Just scared? No. I'm not just scared. See, that makes it sound like some plain old everyday emotion. I'm terrified. Horrified. Overwhelmed with dread. I feel like my brain has been filled full of sewage and I'll never, ever be able to get it clean, like this stuff will eat me alive in my dreams, like I'll never see the world the same again. Scared? They want to eat us, you moron! They want to cut out our hearts and they almost did, you fool! You want to save Senna, go for it, Batman. See you later."

He didn't start walking toward the city. And I didn't start walking away down the beach.

"Look, Testosterone Twins?" April said. "Go

back, don't go back, either way, right now we need to get somewhere where we can rest and sleep and eat and be away from those freaks. We are beat-up, exhausted, worn down. David, you'd be lucky to walk back before you fell asleep in your tracks. So let's compromise, all right? Let's find a safe place."

"I know a safe place," Jalil said. "The real world. Didn't used to think it was safe. Gangs and drugs and racist cops and one thing or another, but I have changed that opinion. Nothing that exists in the greater Chicago metropolitan area is half as bad as what goes on back in that lunatic asylum. If I believed in hell it would be approximately like that city."

"All of Everworld can't be like that," David said.

It began to occur to us that we were moving farther from the ocean, now following the line of the riverbank toward the interior. The river even looked like it might curve back closer to New Tenochtitlan. No one was enthusiastic about that.

The river wasn't impossible to swim, but no one was ready to hand out any guarantees as to the animal life out in that increasingly brown, almost chocolate water. You see jungle, you see water, you think piranha.

Then we came around a spit of land, the last of the dwindling sand, and saw a bridge.

We crouched behind a tree that was far, far too small to hide us. Like four big Sylvesters trying to surprise Tweety Bird.

"Bridge," David said.

"Oh, is that what it is? You know, because I wasn't sure, what with it being this big stone walkway going from one side of a river to the other."

David blushed, embarrassed. "No guards. Not that I can see, anyway."

"Not even with your superpowers?"

This time he just ignored me. "We better move fast. No guards now, but there might be real soon. If they want to cut us off, this is the place."

He was right. He was also annoying. I considered telling him so, but now was not the time for a battle over who was in charge.

We started walking toward the bridge. Then faster. Faster, as the sense of urgency grew, faster, and then we were running, panting with the escape-panic chasing us.

Up onto the bridge, racing one another like all the bogeymen who ever hid in a dark basement were after us.

We reached the far side of the river. Stopped. Looked at one another and laughed sheepishly.

We started walking again. Down the far bank.
Toward the ocean. Jungle to our right. Away from
the city. Away from Senna.

Away from that city of blood and horror. And
as far as I was concerned, I was never going back.

I was cured of the desire to learn what Senna
had in store for me. Cured of that witch.

CHAPTER XVIII

"Yogurt."

I started at the list in my hand. White, college-ruled notebook paper, folded in four.

Yogurt. Coffee filters. Double-A batteries. Toilet paper. Cookies. Liquid hand soap. Ground turkey.

The list was in my left hand. My right hand was on the push bar of a shopping cart. I was standing by the dairy case of the Jewel.

A woman in a long coat stared at me.

"Yogurt," I said.

She looked at me like I might be dangerous. I stared down at the yogurts. So many kinds. So many styles.

"So," I muttered under my breath. "The real world."

I was shopping for my mom. I remembered

her asking me. I remembered that the Real World Christopher hadn't slept much last night because the Real World Christopher knew that Everworld Christopher was getting ready to take a one-way trip to the human butcher shop.

Now RW and EW Christophers became one. I was me, and him. And who was me, and who was him, was impossible to say.

"So. He did fall asleep," I said, referring to EW Christopher. But it felt wrong calling him "he." Like he wasn't me.

It was evening here. My dad had forgotten to pick up the groceries, my mom was working late and wouldn't have time, so, restless, I'd volunteered.

Now here I was in the bright, overlit, too-busy, too-colorful, too-much-going-on-all-around-me grocery store and yet, I knew I was also asleep in the jungle at the edge of an empty beach.

"Excuse me," a middle-aged guy said and made a polite smile.

I pushed my basket out of the way. I needed ground turkey. I moved on to the meat counter and ordered a pound. Big slabs of red and pink and pale meat lay in rows, in mounds, in stacks.

I remembered the ham I'd eaten. I remembered the fact that all the bodies were quickly taken off the battlefield.

Had to be ham. The Aztecs must have pigs, right?

"Pound of ground turkey," I said to the butcher. I was sweating. This body was tired. Not as tired as my other self, but tired. It had been a rough couple of days. Two days here to one over there. The ratio seemed to change. The two universes were not in sync. The cog wheels of time moved in jerks, slips, forward, far forward. Fast, slow.

Two days here since I'd last slept, so briefly, over there. Two days of knowing that I was destined to be a human sacrifice. Two days of wondering, fearing, waiting to suddenly pop out of existence altogether, victim of a murder I'd never see or feel.

"Here you go. Anything else?"

I shook my head. Don't throw up. Don't throw up in the Jewel, Christopher.

I pushed the basket toward the checkout. Long lines. Forget it! Who cared about yogurt and coffee filters and . . . No. No. Don't lose it, Chrisman. Hang in there, Hitchcock. This is the real world. This is where you want to be.

I waited. I glanced at the *National Enquirer* and the *Globe* and the *Sun*. I considered picking up a *TV Guide*.

I had stopped sweating. My heart was calmer. My stomach . . . as long as I didn't think about it.

"Paper or plastic?"

"Plastic," I said. The big choice in the real world: paper or plastic bags.

I paid and pushed the basket out into rain that had made the night fall sooner. Not bad rain. Just enough, and cold enough, to make you want to run.

Over there, the other me was thirsty. We hadn't found water. Or food. Over there my head wound was throbbing. Over there we'd finally just fallen down where we were, dropped to the ground in a small clearing between towering trees.

I was standing watch. Only I wasn't, was I? I was here, which meant I was asleep. The jungle animals could creep up on us anytime. And worse than animals.

I piled the stuff in the back of my Cherokee. I drove home down tree-lined streets.

Home. My house. With the decrepit tree house out back that had been taken over by my little brother. My house, my lawn, the lawn I would have to mow on Saturday. Assuming I was alive and the rain stopped.

I loaded up the groceries, wrapped the handles

of the plastic bags around my wrists, wanting to make it all in one trip. Through the garage, up the deck, through the back door.

"You get the coffee filters?" my dad asked.

I nodded. "Uh-huh."

He was standing by the kitchen island, turning the salad spinner, TV on with the news. He's shorter than me by a couple of inches. The tall genes come from my mom.

"Is Mom home?"

He shook his head. "Not yet. Man, I should have had you pick up some new lettuce; this lettuce is going limp."

"Kind of like you, huh?" I said.

He nodded, accepting the hit. "A) Don't make crude jokes; B) don't make crude jokes about me; and C) come over here and put your hand in the Cuisinart."

My dad and I share a sense of humor. He has a medical supply business. You know, sells stuff to hospitals. I guess he doesn't get a lot of opportunity to be funny at work.

My mom is different. It's not that we're not close. But she works hard. She's a lawyer. Put herself through law school while she was pregnant with my little brother and my dad was being a dog, getting down with his secretary at the Holiday Inn. It all made her a little hard, carrying all that weight, me, my brother, my dad.

She's more serious than me or my dad. Has more of a temper, not that it's her fault. Her job is stressful and sometimes she'll blow up and then, look out. Ten minutes later she's apologizing and rubbing your shoulders and asking if you want a cookie or whatever, but that doesn't change the fact that we all take a step back when she gets that way.

"Is it a major tragedy if I bail on dinner?" I asked.

He gave me the fish eye. "You see that I'm cooking so you run away?"

I shrugged. "Well, there's that. Plus I wanted to hook up with some friends."

He didn't answer right away. "How are you doing, Christopher?"

"What do you mean?"

"I mean the last couple days you've been wandering around here like someone ran over your dog."

"I don't have a dog."

"A figurative dog, not a literal dog."

"I'm fine. It's just this whole heroin addiction thing," I said.

My dad rolled his eyes. "Go. Go chase some

girl and leave your mom and me and Mark to enjoy my world-famous limp salad and grilled chicken."

I laughed. I started to go. But then I didn't. I don't know why. The kitchen just seemed warm and, you know, like my kitchen. My house. Normal.

My dad looked up, saw I was still there. He shot me a questioning look.

"The ladies will just have to wait. I'm not going to let all of you get salmonella and leave me out."

I should find David and April and Jalil. I should check in. Plan. Work something out. Find an escape from our nightmare.

But I didn't want to think about Loki or Huitzilopoctli, trolls or blood-caked priests, Vikings or Aztecs.

I wanted a normal dinner in a normal world. I wanted my dad and my brother and, yeah, I wanted my mommy.

Sitting on the couch watching sitcoms on TV. The definition of normal. When life goes weird on me I touch base with sitcoms. The familiar sets. The familiar sound of laugh track or live audience. The entrances and exits. The pauses as the actors wait for the laugh to build and fade. The familiar setups and payoffs to the jokes.

All that stuff is like part of my DNA. The new and the fairly recent: *Frasier* and *Seinfeld* and *Friends*. The older stuff, *M*A*S*H* and *Mary Tyler Moore* and especially the great, the incomparable *Dick Van Dyke Show*. The stuff is the map to my brain. The foundation of my thinking.

When life becomes surreal, unrecognizable, strange, I go back to the source. Talk to me, Niles; toss off that snobbish line and Frasier will take that Jack Benny reaction shot that milks laughs out of thin air. Talk to me, Tim and the Tool Man; show me that tired, satisfying formula, hah-hah, too much power, better talk to Wilson about it. Phoebe! Monica! Chandler, could you BE more funny? Talk to me, Rob and Laura; make me laugh, make me laugh at all the jokes I've heard and seen a million times before.

Master of your domain. I hate spunk. Rucy, wha are you ap to now? Ohhhh, Rooooob! So no one told you life was gonna be this way, *clapclap-clapclapclap*.

You're the guys I can count on. You're the guys who stay the same, day in, day out.

I clicked back and forth, thumb on the "last channel" button between an old *Mary* and a not-quite-so-old *Friends*. A definite resemblance between Mary Tyler Moore and Courtney Cox. Huh. Never noticed that before.

Stay focused on that, Christopher. Not Loki's son the gigantic wolf, or Huitzilopoctli's priest-killers, or the thousand terrors that even now may be crowding around your sleeping body in a jungle that may be a trillion miles away or right here, in this very room.

The phone rang. I jumped. I tried to ignore it, but it felt bad. Then my mom's voice.

"Christopher! It's for you."

"I'm not home," I yelled.

"It's someone named April, and I'm not paid to lie for you."

"No, you're paid to lie for your clients," I muttered so that she could hear me muttering without hearing what I'd said. I clicked the TV off. "Sorry, Mary, sorry, Monica, gotta go."

I got up and went to the phone in the hallway. "What?" I snapped.

"You fell asleep while you were supposed to be on watch," she accused.

"Sorry. I was tired. Arrest me for dereliction of duty. Are you here or there?"

"I'm here. Jalil took over guard duty, so he's over there and I went back to sleep. David says we should get together. We need to talk. He's at his job at Starbucks. He gets off in an hour."

"I'm busy," I said.

"Busy? Doing what?"

"Watching TV, April. Is that okay? I'm very busy watching TV. So why don't you and David go have your little conference without me?"

Silence. No answer.

"Well, bye, April," I said.

"Christopher, we need to figure a way out of this."

I laughed. "You don't get it, do you? We have no control over the situation. None. We didn't ask to be in this. We had no control. And what do you think we're going to do now? Did you happen to notice an escape hatch when you were playing vestal virgin? Something you didn't tell us about? Because if there's an escape hatch, I'd love to hear about it, but right now, April, I'm going to go back and figure out the mystic connection between Mary and Monica. Good luck, say hi to David for me, that's all."

I slammed down the phone.

My little brother, Mark, was standing on the stairs above me, pretending like he was about to come down but actually spying.

He resumed his descent once he heard me hang up.

"What, are you with the CIA now?" I asked him.

"Don't need to spy, homes, I could have heard you outside."

"'Homes'? 'Homes'? Well, listen up, homey. A) you're a lily-white kid from the upper middle class whose mommy and daddy drive minivans that would match except that one is blue and the other is green, so you are not, repeat, not a streetwise black kid. And B) don't listen to my phone calls."

Mark sneered. "You need to get over this attitude toward black people."

"I don't have an attitude toward black people, I have an attitude toward punks. Punk."

"Yeah, right. Just so happens all your friends are white."

"Hey! It so happens I'm trapped in hell with a black guy, I spent last night with a black guy! I'm sleeping with him right now in —"

I stopped. About two-dozen words too late.

"No way!" Mark yelled, his face a mixture of shock, amazement, gloating, and unease. "Oh, man. Oh, man."

"That came out wrong," I said.

"Oh, man. No, no, that's cool. I'm down with that. That's cool. Each his own, man. I support you. You know, you gotta be what you gotta be, Tinky Winky."

I started to explain. Started to correct. But he was gone, out the door, no doubt to spread the word.

"Not that there's anything wrong with that," I said to his back. A classic *Seinfeld* line.

I had just had a perfect sitcom moment. A classic sitcom setup. Sitcomworld had just intruded into the real world. Surreal. It made me a little uncomfortable. Not as uncomfortable as Fenrir, Loki's bus-sized wolf-son popping into my world had made me, but uncomfortable.

Then I laughed. Sitcom reality was my friend, trying to save me. It had opened its arms to me and wrapped me up in safety. I was good till the next commercial. Good till another me, a faraway me, a me I didn't want to be anymore, woke up.

"Not a sitcom over there, my man," I said to myself, flicking the remote again. "Action-adventure? Horror? Fantasy? Not my fantasy."

I hit the remote. The credits were rolling beside a promo for a lame Steven Seagall movie.

I was part of the cast of a movie directed by lunatic immortals. I was one of the actors. Question was, was I the hero? Or was I the guy they kill off early to give the audience a good fear-rush?

"No, that's not the question, either. The question is, 'How the hell do I get out of this movie?'"

CHAPTER
XX

I was asleep in my bed when I awoke in Everworld.

I lay there confused. Lost. Looked for the num-
bers on my clock. Looked for the faint outline of
my window. For the line of light under my door
cast by the night-light in the hallway. None of
the above.

I felt like crying. I didn't want to be here.

Suddenly a hand clamped over my mouth.
Soft hand. April's luminous eyes just inches above
mine. A finger over her mouth. A silent, voice-
less, "Shhh."

I nodded. She took her hand away.

Jalil lay nearby, on his stomach, awake, alert. I
was on my back. Not the best way to deal with an
attack.

I strained to hear what was happening. The

sounds of the nocturnal forest. The breeze rustling tall branches, the unsettling sounds of tiny things creeping and crawling beneath the fallen leaves. And something more purposeful.

Whatever it was, it wasn't afraid. It wasn't creeping. Wasn't stopping to listen. It moved confidently, swiftly, quietly.

Toward us.

I saw David off to my right, gripping his sword, kneeling, poised, tensed. I rolled over, ever so quietly. Fumbled in the darkness, feeling for my ax. I couldn't find it, fought down the panic, felt around more methodically, grabbed April's ankle instead, didn't want her ankle, wanted my ax, wanted something I could use, man, something I could use to kill, stay alive.

Welcome back to Everworld, Christopher Hitchcock.

"Sounds like more than one," Jalil whispered.

"More than one what?" I muttered.

Whoever was moving stopped. I froze. All but my fingers, which kept up their blind search for the ax. Got it! Fingers tightened around it, security, God knows not much, but some. I never wanted to be without a weapon in Everworld again.

And then, a chill that shivered my back. I felt

something land on my shoulder. Not heavy. Small. Alive. Something definitely alive.

A needle-sharp point pressed against the side of my neck. A poke, a threat, a warning. Something sharp pressed against an artery.

"If friends, no fear," a flutey voice said from the darkness. Not from whatever was on my shoulder. "If foe, fear."

"Friends," I said, ordering myself not to move, not to move a millimeter.

"Show," the odd voice said.

I stayed very still. I didn't know what was sticking me in the neck. Didn't know if it was dangerous, deadly, or just painful, but there is something about a dagger's point against your flesh, against the prickling, goose-bumped flesh that stretches so ineffectually over the pulsing jugular vein that concentrates all your attention.

"They want us to show ourselves," Jalil said.

"Something . . . is poking . . . my neck," I said.

"Stay ready," David warned. "Stand up slowly."

I stood up slowly. The needle point stayed with me. I didn't let go of my ax. Didn't try to use it, either. You don't want to use an ax to swat something on your neck.

"We're friends," April said in her gentlest, talking-to-rabid-dogs voice.

"Whose?" the voice asked. Amused.

"Whose friends? Um . . . we're one another's friends. We'll be your friends if you don't mean us any harm."

"Light," the voice said, and instantly the woods around us were illuminated by a dozen wobbly, wavering lights, each perhaps as bright as a candle. In the pitch-black it seemed pretty bright.

Bright enough to show me that we were a lot worse off than we thought. They were all around us. What I had taken to be one or maybe a few creatures moving quietly was in fact twenty or twenty-five creatures, each the size of a man.

The size of a man. And that was it for resemblance to anything I'd ever seen before. They were dark gray as well as I could tell in the shadows. Maybe six feet tall, but closer to twelve feet long from nose to toes. Or from nose to tail.

The face was a long, very long, maybe three-foot-long point, a hard cone, a needle, like an anteater who'd evolved to hunt for ants inside of concrete. Resting above, at the back of the needle were two eyes, enormous, blue-irised within dark red.

The rest of the body was a sort of a cramped letter C. The body arched from nose down to claw feet, so that the sharp talon toes were almost directly beneath the point of the snout. It had a sort of short tail or long fin halfway around the arc to provide some kind of balance.

Two legs thrust forward, two brawny arms at mid-arc, two smaller, delicate arms jutting out just below the eyes.

That was most of them, the big ones. But there were the others. Smaller, miniature versions, but with gossamer wings. One of these was resting comfortably on my shoulder, with its six-inch version of the needle mouth pressed against my neck.

The candle lights were coming from the bellies of the little ones. Fireflies the size of pigeons.

The nearest of the big ones walked toward us. It was an impossible movement. A balancing act with each step. A leg stretched out, almost telescoping out, with loose-fitting gray flesh unwrinkling. The foot would touch down, balance would be reestablished, then the other foot would come forward, very slowly.

We could run and there was no way these things were going to catch us. Then, as if reading my mind, one of the lights, the little ones, jerked toward David. David had twitched. The little one had covered twenty feet before David could go from start of twitch to end of twitch.

I did a quick, desperate brain-search. What

were these things? What dark myth had these monsters crawled out of?

But I knew: There was nothing human here. Man's gods and demons and monsters are always mostly human. Distorted in form or power, but mostly human.

I sucked in a deep breath. "Who are you people?"

CHAPTER XXI

"We are Coo-Hatch of the Third Forge. You?"

"Um . . . humans," I said.

The main Coo-Hatch blinked slowly. "Two legs, two arms, small eyes, fur on head, clothed. Human," he said, adding an unspoken but implied 'duh.' "Which humans?"

"We're minstrels," David said. "Traveling entertainers. I'm David. That's April, Jalil, and Christopher."

I couldn't believe David remembered our cover story. Minstrels. Yeah. It worked with the Vikings. But the Vikings were party animals by nature. These guys didn't look like they'd really care for any drinking songs.

The Coo-Hatch used one of his tiny uppermost hands to point at my ax, at David's sword. "Viking weapons. Poor steel. I am Estett."

Jalil said, "The Coo-Hatch. I remember the Vikings, when they were asking us about the Hetwan and Loki? They mentioned the Coo-Hatch."

"Sven Swordeater said they trade with the Coo-Hatch for steel," David recalled.

"Not Coo-Hatch steel," the weird thing named Estett said, eyeing our weapons again with unmistakable distaste. "Lend."

He held out his hand for my ax. It had been mere moments since I swore never to give up my weapon. I handed it to him anyway.

Estett used one of his medium arms to test the balance of my ax, then threw it, twirling, end over end. It thunked into a tree and quivered there.

"Viking steel," he said with no effort to hide his condescension.

Then he opened a slit in the skin of his flank, and I realized for the first time that it was some kind of clothing. With one of his middle arms he drew out what looked like a small airplane propeller, a foot in diameter, with the blades bent back and a round hole in the center. The steel shone in the dim light. Glittered. Like it was radioactive. Maybe it was.

With feline speed, the Coo-Hatch threw the weapon. It flew through the air, twirling, level, sliced into a tree, through a tree, so fast, so easily that the tree stood still, poised, needing a fresh breeze before it began to fall.

The tree fell straight toward us, fifty feet of bare trunk before it spread into branches. Right toward us.

"Run!" David yelled. But before we could react, before we could do more than flash on some red-plaid lumberjack yelling, "Timber!" the rest of the Coo-Hatch struck.

With no word spoken, no evidence of haste, no sign of concern, but with easy, liquid grace, the other Coo-Hatch all drew similar weapons and sent them flying.

The tree's trunk, already at a sharp angle and accelerating down toward my head, was sliced into two dozen separate logs.

The logs fell. The Coo-Hatch didn't move. And some subconscious instinct for survival kept us all rooted, too.

Like mortar shells, the logs fell around us. Each log was a neat two or three feet long. Each impact made the ground jump. Bruised my soles and rattled my knees. The branches fell far behind us.

The spinning propellers all arced back toward their owners, who caught them on their needle noses or mouths or whatever they were. It was a disconcertingly comical thing to see.

I decided not to laugh.

"Coo-Hatch steel," Estett said with evident satisfaction.

It could have been a threat. As a threat it was a pretty good one. The message was so, so clear: We can make you into salami.

But I had a feeling maybe scaring us wasn't the point. My dad's a salesman. I know salesmen.

"Pretty good," I said. "So how much do they cost?"

CHAPTER
XXII

The Coo-Hatch led us through the darkness before dawn. We followed. Quiet. Not terrified, but nervous. I wondered if there was ever going to be a moment in Everworld when I wasn't at least nervous.

They were strange creatures, that's for sure. But strange as they were, dangerous as they could clearly be, they didn't give me the sick pit-of-the-stomach dread I felt when facing a simple, dirty Aztec priest. For one thing, they'd chopped up a tree. Not one of us.

For another thing, it was hard to take that bizarre walk of theirs without wanting to giggle. Sort of like an exaggerated Groucho walk. Funny. There was no avoiding it, it was funny.

I guess Jalil saw me grinning. "Here's a suggestion: Don't laugh at them. Or if you do, go stand far away from me."

"They seem nice enough."

"You're not even nice enough," Jalil said darkly.

They led us to a stream, barely visible in the light cast by the hovering bird-creatures. We could hear it gurgling and chuckling like any stream in the real world. But it was concealed by high-grown ferns and palms and weeds.

The Coo-Hatch made a clearing. They used their throwing blades. It took about three seconds. They turned the overgrown weeds into a lawn. We could have played a game of croquet.

They made a fire by striking sparks from a chunk of rock and a small triangle of steel.

"Not Coo-Hatch steel," Estett explained, indicating the triangle. "Coo-Hatch steel cuts rock."

Then all of us, Coo-Hatch and human, sat down around a modest fire and crossed our legs.

It felt okay, weirdly enough. Sitting with a bunch of aliens in the middle of a jungle in the night. Odd to be more at ease with a bunch of aliens, a bunch of off-world freaks than the Aztecs, or, for that matter, some of the Vikings. But "odd" was the synonym for "normal" in Everworld.

I almost wished the Aztecs would come after us

and have these boys demonstrate their blades on them. I wished that a lot.

"What now? We sing 'Kumbaya'?" David whispered.

"Now we do business," I said.

"Why?"

"Because that's what these guys want to do," I said. "They're salesmen, can't you tell?"

David nodded. "Fair enough. I don't need to be sliced and diced. We do what they want."

"What do we have to trade?" April asked. "And what are we buying?"

"I wouldn't mind having one of those throwing knives," Jalil said.

"I still have the stuff in my backpack," April said. She swung if off her shoulder and onto her lap. "Advil? I have Advil. The CD player. Maybe they'd be interested in that."

She was pulling things out one by one. The rest of us were reaching under our various Viking-issue animal skins to dig in our jeans pockets.

The Coo-Hatch were staring. I watched the royal-blue irises within the bulbous red eyes. The blue expanded and contracted. But mostly there was no response. The expressions seemed easy enough to understand. Mostly indifference. No reaction to a bottle of Advil.

"Let's see if they'll sell us Manhattan for twenty-four dollars' worth of beads," I said.

Item after item. April emptied her bag, then we started emptying our pockets. We still had a lot of keys. Useless. I'd had to get myself a spare for use on the other side, back in the real world. The Coo-Hatch looked at the keys, tested the metal, shrugged, handed them back.

They were marginally more interested in Jalil's thin Swiss Army knife. They sneered at the steel, of course. Not impolite, just like, "Yeah, big deal." But they liked the idea, the mechanism. They opened the tiny blade and the tiny screwdriver.

"They come bigger sometimes," Jalil explained. "Several blades, Phillips, corkscrews, scissors, saw, so on."

Estett nodded, a very human gesture. "Poor steel, but interesting." He shot a sidelong look at some of his people. I had a feeling that if we ran into the Coo-Hatch a few months down the road they'd be offering little Coo-Hatch Army knives for sale.

A slight glimmer of reaction to the CD player. The Coo-Hatch touched it. Then pushed it away contemptuously.

More keys. A felt-tip pen. No reaction.

Two books.

No reaction.

"Wait," April said. She reached across me to grab the top book. *Chemistry: Principles and Application.*

She flipped through the pages. Then went to the index. Then went to a particular page. She opened the book and held it out for Estett.

Red eyes stared. Then . . .

"Ah!"

The Coo-Hatch almost snatched for the book, then caught himself. "Lend? Examine?"

"Sure," April said. She handed the book to the alien.

Estett turned the pages reverently. He held it with his middle arms and turned the pages with his upper, delicate arms. He kept turning. Then, looking embarrassed, he closed the book reluctantly and handed it back.

"What did you show him?" I asked April.

"A description of the steel-making process."

"Trade?" Estett asked.

"What do you have on the table, dude?" I asked him.

He considered. "Fix small red knife."

"It's not broken." Jalil said.

"Weapons," David interrupted greedily. "We want the throwing blades."

Estett may have laughed. Sounded like a laugh. It shouldn't have, though. Not with that mouth, that throat. Then again, he was speaking English, and reading English, so who was I to object to the fact that his laugh sounded almost human?

"Three years' training to master the throwing blade," Estett said. "Handle wrong way, no fingers, no arm. Drop, no foot. Throw badly, no house, many die. Coo-Hatch do not sell weapons. Sell tools. Humans do not need more weapons."

"Hey, I need more weapons," I said. "This human sure needs some serious heat. You want to know where I've been lately? I could use artillery, let alone a knife."

David's eyes glinted angrily. "Estett, what we want is the —"

April interrupted, putting a hand on his arm. "He's right, David. You've never used a weapon like that. It'd be like giving a machine gun to a little kid."

"Ouch."

"I never used a sword, either, but I figured it out," David argued.

"Swords don't cut through trees, David. You think you're going to grab one of those blades and go back after Senna? You'd kill yourself or me. Or her. Or a bunch of innocent people."

"There are no innocent people in that city," Jalil muttered. "But April's right. So is Estett," he added, with a nod to the alien. "A weapon that wild and dangerous, you'd need to know exactly what you're doing. Takes these guys three years to learn how to throw one? Let it go, David."

"Well, what are they going to trade us, then?" David demanded.

"How about we ask them?" April said, obviously annoyed at David's continuing display of attitude.

"Okay, if they won't give us the throwing knives, how about a ticket to the Bahamas and three weeks at a fabulous resort with hot and hotter running bikini babes?" I suggested.

"Steel secrets very old. Good steel would be made from book, but not Coo-Hatch steel," Estett said, pointing at the book.

"He's dissing the merchandise. Ah, so we bargain, eh?" I said.

April shook her head. "He's just pointing out the obvious. What, you think that book has some formula for making better steel than these guys can make? Get real. It's something else he saw in there. Or maybe it's all of it. Either way, I wouldn't mind getting rid of that book — it weighs a ton."

"What do you offer?" Jalil asked the Coo-Hatch.

"Coo-Hatch steel."

"Are we going in circles here?"

The Coo-Hatch don't smile. Couldn't, probably. I never did see its mouth. Not for sure. "Show knife. Small red knife."

Jalil fished for his knife again and handed it to Estett.

Estett opened the blade. "Poor steel. Coo-Hatch steel better."

CHAPTER
XXIII

"Oh, this is good," I said. "What was that sword in King Arthur? You know, his magic sword or whatever?"

"Excalibur," Jalil supplied.

"Yeah. That's it. So our Excalibur is going to be some two-inch-blade Swiss Army knife? Great. Hold up there, Big H, while I unsnap my teeny-tiny knife and trim your evil toenails. Yo, Loki, call your monster wolf-son back or I swear I'll shave off some of his fur!"

"It's more than we have right now," David said. He was pissed, obviously. He wanted some big, nasty firepower, same as me. In the land of the sword, the man with the Glock is king.

"Should we really be giving them all the information that may be in that book?" Jalil wondered.

"What, you don't want to violate the Prime Directive, Spock?" I said. "So they learn how to make cleaning solution. Who cares?"

"There are explosives in that book," Jalil whispered. "Or at least that can be extrapolated."

"Don't use words like 'extrapolated,' Jalil; it's not necessary, we all know you're smarter than we are. And who cares? So they make plastique and go around blowing up buildings. I don't care about this place! This place isn't my home, all right?"

Jalil gave me one of his sideways looks. "You're not finding Everworld scary enough? You want to spread around some new weapons information? I'm not talking 'Save the Aztecs' here, I'm looking at me walking down some street somewhere in this little universe and getting blown away because I wanted a cool knife."

April smiled at Estett. "We need to consider this for just a few seconds." She turned to us and in a low voice said, "Look, I'm sick of carrying the book, anyway; it weighs a ton. Besides, have any of you considered what they might do if we just refuse to trade? I mean, maybe that's like a mortal insult to the Coo-Hatch."

This put a new light on things. I saw a mental picture of a Coo-Hatch blade bisecting me so neatly, so smoothly that the two halves of me would continue alive for a while, blood pumping through arteries, nerves communicating across the minuscule gap, me realizing I'd been chopped in two, trying to use my hands to hold onto my stomach and keep my bottom half attached.

Too easy to picture, that was. I'd seen it in living color, or something close, when Huitzilopoctli's mirror made one Sven Swordeater into two.

"I'm thinking, let's not make anyone mad," I said.

"We do the deal," David said.

"Hey, hey, back up there, Saddam. You don't give the orders here."

He looked surprised. "I'm agreeing with you."

"Fine, then say, 'I agree with Christopher,' not 'We do it,' General Jerkwad."

"What's climbed up your butt now?"

I jabbed a finger at David's face. "You're not the hero of this story and the rest of us your faithful followers. The hero lives, the best friend gets killed. The rules of the form, man. You're not the hero of this movie, so back up."

David rolled his eyes. "He's having a breakdown. What is it they call it? Post-traumatic stress something syndrome? You having flashbacks about the pyramid, Christopher? You seeing obsidian knives?"

"Ignore them." April smiled at Estett. She took the knife from Jalil's hands, lifted the book up off her lap, and handed both to the Coo-Hatch. "Deal," she said.

It took the Coo-Hatch an hour. They took our little campfire and began blowing into it with their needle mouths. Out of rucksacks and their pouches came various bits of lumpy-looking material, stuff that could be dirt clods for all I knew. They worked. Banged. Blew. Collected water in a little trench they dug from the stream.

April found what may have been, could have been a Coo-Hatch female. She went off and had some girl-talk time. David and Jalil and I just moped and watched the Coo-Hatch and wondered how our lives had brought us here.

After a while, and with gray light beginning to outline the treetops above us, the Coo-Hatch handed the knife to Jalil, still warm to the touch, along with a lot of warnings like, "Don't test it on your finger or you'll be counting in base nine, you idiot human." Or words to that effect.

Then they took off, the big Grouchos, the little Tinkerbells; they just walked into the woods carrying a high-school chemistry textbook and reading it by the light of the gray dawn.

We were alone.

April looked grim.

"What's up?" I asked her.

She shook her head. "I was talking to the Coo-Hatch. They're here like us. I mean, they didn't ask to be here, they were carried here by some god of the fire and goddess of the ore or whatever, it was hard to make sense of. Anyway, it was a century ago. They've been trying to find their way back to their own universe ever since. Talking about their families and all, their villages, their forges and mines and so on. They're lonely."

"Trying to get out of here for a hundred years?" Jalil asked.

April shrugged. "That's what they say. There are seven groups of Coo-Hatch wandering around Everworld. A hundred years. They can't get back. Stuck here."

She was acting tough, but there were tears in her eyes and she was swallowing too much. April wanted to go home. So did I. In about ten seconds I was going to bust out crying, too.

"That doesn't mean we're stuck here," I said, doing my best heroic, "never say die," "on to the summit!" voice.

I looked to David for support on that, but David's face was carefully neutral.

Of course, I thought. That's good news for the glory dog. David never wanted to go home.

"A hundred years," April said.

"Yeah."

Jalil opened the knife very, very carefully, as we'd been warned. He found a sapling maybe two inches thick. He cut it once, with an effortless movement, almost a flick of the wrist. With a second reach-around cut, the sapling fell.

"Well," I said. "We have the Magic Toenail Clipper of Power! We have Ex-freaking-calibur. Let us go forth and conquer."

CHAPTER
XXIV

"I'm starving. I'm thirsty," I said.

"Yeah, well, talking about it every five minutes, that'll make it better," Jalil said.

We were on the beach again. Out of the jungle. Standing there. Just standing. Lost. Confused. Depressed. Mad. Mostly mad.

The Coo-Hatch story hung over us. A hundred years they'd been trying to find a way out of this universe, this bubble in a bubble, this pocket of madness.

If they couldn't get out, how were we going to get out?

The reality was setting in. There might be no way out. This might be it. This could be our lives now. A few hours in the real world and a lifetime here.

From the start of it all we'd kept going on adrenaline, and then relief at having escaped the obsidian knife. But we were tired. Past tired, all of us. And more lost than any four humans have ever been before.

The sun was up and with it the heat and humidity. If we stayed on the beach, our unprotected faces would blister. If we went back into the shade of the jungle, the bugs would eat us alive.

Fear, hunger, thirst, heat, hopelessness, and a simmering, undirected anger that was all the hotter for having no clear target. I was ripe for a fight. David had worn out my last remaining nerve.

An explosion had to come. Sooner or later. We were up against the decision of what to do, and I knew, knew, knew what David wanted. Knew it and was determined to stop him, and, while I was at it, to haul him down off his throne for good. The jumped-up junior general, I wasn't taking that anymore.

If I were a more mature person, a better person, I'd have tried hard to avoid a fight. But that's not me. I was OD'ing on the rage that grows out of fear. I wanted to hit, to hurt, to scream and threaten and flail around like a toddler having a temper tantrum. I was trapped and powerless. Helpless.

"I am starving," I complained. "It's a toss-up as to which I want more: a drink or a meal. Both would be nice. Isn't there supposed to be fruit on the trees in the jungle? Palm trees with coconuts or bananas or whatever?"

"We're well within foraging range for the Aztecs in the city back there," Jalil pointed out. "They were thin, as you might have noticed. Hungry. If there were fruit on the trees, they'd have picked it, probably did pick it already. You'd probably have figured that out yourself, Christopher, if you'd quit whining long enough to process a thought."

In a millisecond I switched gears from being ready to kill David to being ready to kill Jalil.

"Don't piss me off, Jalil, just don't, okay? Because I am plenty pissed off. You aren't going to like what happens next if you keep it up. Fair warning."

Jalil glared at me, his mouth twisted with bitter anger. "You know, I'm here in the nuthouse with crazy killer gods and alien steel salesmen and alcoholic Vikings and cannibal Aztecs, and despite all that, the biggest pain in my butt is some big, dumb cracker. Now, why is that?"

"Cracker? Now it's racial stuff? You want to start throwing words around, Jalil? Jalil, what's that, Muslim for —"

"That's it, all over," David said, stepping in between us. "You shut up." He pointed a finger in my face.

That was it. The fuse had burned all the way down.

"Hey, maybe you need to figure out which side you're on, David!" I yelled. "You want to throw down with me to save the 'brutha'?"

At the same time Jalil was yelling, "Back off, David, I don't need the Hebrew army to help me deal with this racist piece of —"

David emitted a short, harsh laugh, put up his hands, and backed up. "Forget both of you."

After that it was just me and Jalil yelling, shouting, chest-pushing, shoving.

"You want to do this? Let's do it!" I yelled, my face an inch from Jalil's.

My hand went to my ax. Jalil's was on his long dagger. Face-to-face, the two of us. Sweat popping out of tight skin, eyes bulging, lips stretched over bared teeth, chests out.

"You know what?" April said to David. "Let them fight. The three of you, it's all you know how to do. So here's the thing, you two fight, then David fights the winner."

I barely heard her. All I saw was Jalil, all I heard was his ragged breathing, poised, ready to explode with violence on his first move.

Stupid. I did know that. It was David I was mad at, not Jalil. But at the moment logic was a tiny, faraway voice way, way back in my head. Up front, filling all of the rest of my skull was panic — fear and fury.

April came over and pushed her way between us. Ludicrous, of course, I noted that way back somewhere in my head. I did know it was an absurd picture, me and Jalil making a sandwich of April.

"Okay, look," April said. "I'm tired of trying to get the three of you *boys* to behave like adults. I don't know, maybe males aren't capable of ever really being adults. Maybe you're crippled by your hormones or something."

I turned on April. "You know what, I'm sick of your 'better-than-everyone, my crap doesn't stink' attitude. In case you missed it, this isn't Political Correctness World, okay? So why don't you go sit over there, out of danger, like you sat on your butt on the ship while the men were taking care of business back, back . . . then. Day before yesterday. The battle and all."

I was babbling. I knew I was babbling. Didn't care. I wanted to hurt someone. I wanted to hurt someone so badly. But April was looking up at me from an inch away, and mad as she was, there was this mocking thing going on. She was laughing at me. At both of us.

"Not worth the bruised fists," Jalil sneered at me and stepped back suddenly.

I stepped back at the same moment. April took a deep breath, ran a hand back through her hair, and straightened her top.

Jalil was pressing his hands against the side of his head like maybe the left half and right half had come unglued. "Look what's happened to me, man. What I said, David, that was uncalled for. I'd take that moment back if I could."

"It's been a slightly tense week," David said. "Forget about it."

"Look what's happened to me," Jalil repeated, oblivious to David's answer. He wiped sweat from his forehead with the back of his hand and stared at his wet hand like he'd just noticed the early signs of leprosy.

"Yeah, well, I'm not some kind of racist, either," I said, huffy, still trying to sound mad and tough. "That's bull."

"Okay, line up," April said.

"What?"

"Line up. The three of you. You, too, David. Shoulder to shoulder, right there, line up, just do

it!" Her voice rose to a yell on the last three
words.

We lined up.

April stood in front of us, hands on hips.
"Look, you need each other. I need you, all of
you. And, since I did happen to save your worth-
less, pathetic lives, all three of you, I think it's fair
to say you need me. So I don't care what stupid-
ity you have hidden away inside your heads, that
has to be it for this kind of thing. The four of us
are all any of us has. We are in it deep here. We're
in it so deep we may never get out. So basically,
and I say this with respect and affection: behave.
Behave like civilized human beings, and if you
boys can't figure out what that means, ask me and
I'll tell you. From now on, if we have disagree-
ments, we have a vote, majority rule, and if it's a
tie we do what I say."

She said the word "boy" in a way that made it
sound belittling and yet was somehow sexy.

"Will you spank me if I'm bad?" I asked, bat-
ting my eyes.

"No," she shot back. "But if any of you want to
fight again, I'm going to let you fight. No
weapons. Bare fists. And bare bodies, too, like the
ancient Greeks."

"Say what?" David said.

She flashed her provocative April grin. "I

mean, I have to get some entertainment out of this."

We all laughed. Moment passed. Rage burned out. We were still lost and scared, but not quite homicidal anymore.

Still, it took me twenty minutes or so before I got around to saying anything to Jalil. And when I did it was to ask if he thought we should go deeper into the jungle to find food.

Not exactly an apology. Neither of us ever did that.

CHAPTER
XXV

We trekked into the jungle again and found the stream where we'd met the Coo-Hatch. We drank. Wasted time. Back where we'd started. Nothing accomplished but a stupid fight.

We hadn't even gotten to the main issue: Where were we going? We all knew that would be a fight and our peace was still pretty tenuous. But in the end, there was no avoiding it. We stayed or we moved. If we moved, we needed a direction.

"Okay," I said, after taking a moment to enjoy the sight of April leaning far over into the stream, "unless we're planning to set up house-keeping here we'd better figure out where we're going. What we're doing."

April stood up and wiped her mouth. "Where's David?"

Jalil shrugged. "Saw him heading back toward the beach. Figured he wanted a P.M."

P.M. Private Moment. That's what we'd started calling the need to disappear behind the bushes for some basic biological functioning.

"David!" April yelled.

I had a sudden sinking sensation. The feeling you get when you've guessed something you really hope isn't true.

I jumped up and started plowing through foliage toward the beach.

"What are you doing?" Jalil yelled after me.

"David, man, he's taken off."

"What do you mean? Where would he . . . Oh, man!"

We found fresh footprints on the beach. Running-shoe tread. And there, in the damp sand near the shore, he'd written with the tip of his sword.

We stood there staring at the four words outlined in foot-tall sand letters: *Going back for her.*

The three of us spent about thirty seconds running through our vocabularies of curses, insults, and threats.

"Now what?" I demanded.

"Now we deal with the choice David has left us: Go after him or go on alone," Jalil said.

I shook my head. "This sucks. Maybe he is the

hero of this story. But that can't be, man. We have to walk away, let him go off on his own. Otherwise, what are we? We're supporting actors, that's what. We're dead."

Jalil favored me with his sideways look, a look I now saw had a strange similarity to that of Huitzilopoctli. "What are you babbling about, and I ask that as a friend?"

"Any movie you ever see, man, the hero survives. He's got a best friend, a babe, and a black guy. Sometimes the best friend is the black guy. Don't you ever go to the movies? The best friend and the black guy? Dead meat. Dead freaking meat. Even the babe if there's going to be a sequel. Like a Bond movie or whatever. That bear movie? That Baldwin brother and that other guy, the old one, and they're all alone except for, ta-da, the black guy, and who does the bear eat? Not the Baldwin brother."

Jalil nodded. "Uh-huh. Again, I want to say this as a friend, and with no racial animosity, because it's not about you being a redneck, all right? But you, Christopher, you are an idiot."

"You ever see Schwarzenegger get killed?" I shrilled.

"Yeah, *Terminator Two*. *Terminator One*, too."

"He was a robot!"

"Okay, let me waste some more minutes of my

life to figure out what your malfunction is. You think life runs according to the way it does in action movies? The hero lives, everyone else is expendable."

"I'm just saying, David's off playing tough guy. He's Clint, we're standing around here with our fingers in our noses."

"Clint Eastwood didn't go off after some psycho chick," Jalil argued. "The hero doesn't do that stuff unless it's like some kid's fairy tale."

"Prince Charming," I spat bitterly.

"Jalil's right," April said. "Face it, David's not heroic. He's just obsessed." She bit her lip, thoughtful. "Or not obsessed. Not obsessed — under a spell."

It came out sounding so natural. Like nothing important had been said. But I knew it was important. It was the first time any of us had ever talked like maybe, maybe it was true. Maybe Senna wasn't the girl we all thought we knew. Maybe she really was something inexplicable. Something magic.

Jalil threw up his hands. "Am I the only rational human being here? Hey, hey, it's the twenty-first century; this is not the Dark Ages. It's not even the sixties. One of you thinks life works like the plots of the crap you find in the action-adventure aisle at Blockbuster, and the other thinks what? Magic spells and potions?"

He rounded on April. "What happened? Senna put the whammy on David? Cast a voodoo spell? Now he's drawn to her because she has some magical power over him?"

Jalil threw up his hands. Literally. Then looked up at the sky and muttered something about inventing his own universe so he could crawl inside.

A spell? Crazy. Of course it was. But in my mind I was back at that pool party. Feeling like I'd never noticed Senna before. Feeling like suddenly I couldn't notice anyone else.

I felt a shiver. How did you know when you were under a spell? My gaze refocused. Refocused on April's green eyes. Her expression was angry. Suspicious.

"Why were we all there?" April asked me. "Why were we all down at the lake, standing around there, drawn there, waiting, watching Senna? Why? How did that happen? How about you, Jalil? Why were you there? You have some rational explanation for why you were there?"

Jalil took a step back. His face blanked.

"Yeah, what were you doing there, Jalil?" I asked. "Me, I was going out with Senna. Then

David was with her. April's her half sister. What about you, man? What did you and the witch have going on?"

"I don't know why I was there that morning," Jalil admitted. But that must have been too much like he was agreeing with us because then he said, "Maybe I just woke up early and was restless. Felt like going for a drive."

"You ever do that before? Get up that early and suddenly decide to take a drive down to the lake?" April pressed.

Jalil didn't answer. He sidestepped the question and pushed back at us with sarcasm. "It's not exactly bizarre behavior, you know. People do drive down to the lake. That's why they have parking, so people can drive down there."

I felt the cold creeps crawling across my flesh. We'd been in one crap storm after another since showing up in Everworld. There hadn't been time to think. No time to really ask the basic questions.

Why were we here? Why had we been drawn to Senna at the very moment when she could pull us into this madness?

April laughed without humor. "David's not the hero. He's just a fool. A puppet. Like all of us. This is all Senna. It's all her. This is her game we're playing. We're all fools."

We stood there, the three of us, each hiding his own little secrets, each nursing his own little grudge. Each with his own superstitions, even Jalil. Maybe especially Jalil, holding on with a death grip to a philosophy that belonged to a whole different universe.

Although, I had to admit, it was hard to be much crazier than believing the world ran according to the neat, predictable rules of sitcoms and action movies.

April whispered something. I couldn't hear it. I don't think I was supposed to. Then she started walking.

"Where are you going?" Jalil demanded. "Are you going after David?"

"No. I'm going after Senna."

CHAPTER XXVI

New Tenochtitlan. Not a place I'd ever thought I'd see again. Not a place I wanted to see again.

We knew the way back. Easy to find. All we had to do was follow the beach. Over the bridge, then follow the beach to the burned-out Viking ships, hang a left across the battlefield where Olaf and Sven had died. We knew the way.

And even if memory had not shown us the way, the neat imprints of running shoes on sand would have been roadmap enough.

We walked till we could see the river's mouth turning the beach inward toward the bridge. But then the trail of running-shoe waves cut left, inland. Into the jungle. The trees were smaller, more stunted here, closer to the city. The forest seemed dead. Scarcely a bird to cry at our approach. Nothing but bugs the size of rats and rats the size of spaniels.

It was harder following David's track through the jungle, looking for the crushed weeds, the occasional clear footprint in mud.

Thirst was back. Hunger, too. We were pampered products of a well-ordered world, after all. Three meals and between-meal snacks and a faucet or a bottle of Dannon spring water there for the taking.

I was sweaty and slashed by thorns and whipped by weeds and muddy and the gash on my head was itching and I kept having to touch it to be sure something wasn't crawling into it.

It was a toss-up who I hated more right then: David for being a weak-willed fool, Jalil for being a tiresome know-it-all with a chip on his shoulder, April for so clearly not having the least little interest in me. Or Senna for seducing me, enthralling me, trapping me in this schizophrenic's vision.

Putting a spell on me.

Or maybe I was just mad at good old Christopher. I was whiny, bitchy, snide, resentful, childish. Picking stupid fights. Acting like the kind of person I couldn't stand.

That's not the way it was supposed to be. That wasn't the movie in my head. That wasn't the fantasy. I was on an adventure, wasn't I? I was supposed to stand tall and keep my jaw clenched and my eyes steely, and laugh at danger and laugh at difficulty and never show a flicker of emotion, and triumph and get the girl — that was the picture, that was the script.

Instead I was wandering around, waiting for the next nightmare to come popping up out of nowhere and do to me what Huitzilopoctli had done to King Olaf.

Then again, I was alive. Olaf was dead. Maybe Olaf should have complained more and spent less time being bold and brave.

We were walking uphill now, which was just great because if there's anything more obnoxious than walking through untracked jungle with your dirty clothes glued to your body by a combination of heat and humidity so high you could cook a lobster, it's doing it while struggling against gravity.

"Loki and Huitzilopoctli and the rest of these stupid gods create this universe and can't dial the gravity down a few notches, make it easier for people?" I muttered.

Suddenly we emerged into a clearing. A clearing atop a hill maybe three hundred feet tall. Not exactly Mount Everest, but taller than the surrounding countryside.

David was standing with his back to us, on top of a mossy rock.

"Oh, look, it's Lewis and/or Clark," I said. I shouted, "Hey! Hey! We've been looking for you."

David glanced back over his shoulder. Then turned away again. "I heard you coming."

April and Jalil walked over and climbed up on the rock. So what was I supposed to do? I went and climbed up. Four of us on a big rock.

I could see quite a bit from up there. The city, mostly, the pyramid, like I needed a refresher on that. But I could also see the beach and the jungle beyond the city, too. A volcano far off, inland. A hint of a distant river. And on my right, the ocean or sea, or really big lake, whatever it was.

I cringed at the sight of the city. If I could see it, maybe Huitzilopoctli could see me. I guess we were a mile from the pyramid. Not one percent of the minimum distance I wanted between me and Big H.

My eyes slid away, then back. Tried to look away, but how could I when he might even now be looking at me?

There was smoke rising from the city. Cooking fires, I assumed. Then I saw the mass of people moving away from the city. They were leaving by a far gate, heading away from us into the jungle.

"'Fugees," April said.

At least that's what I heard. It took me a minute to track. 'Fugees. Refugees.

"Yeah," David agreed. "The city is emptying out. I've been trying to count, or at least make a guess. Thousands of them. Maybe everyone in the city."

"Maybe everyone," he said again.

Chapter
XXVII

It took us two hours to reach the city, the gate we'd arrived through as prisoners. Might have gone quicker but my feet were dragging. My brain may have been dumb enough to go there, but my body was doing everything it could to hold me back.

Not much had changed in the city. Except there was no one home. The streets were empty. Not a man, woman, or child. Not a soldier or priest.

Here and there, a smashed pot or out-of-place chair in the middle of the street. Simple things made eerie by where they shouldn't be. An Aztec robe ruffled by the slight breeze. A shattered Aztec sword. A primitive doll or statuette, head crushed.

Smoke drifted from windows. Old fires, mostly burned down now.

There were no bodies. None. Aztec, Viking, someone, lots of someones had died but there were no bodies. Just blood. Smeared against walls. Puddled on pavement. Dried stains marking windows where life-and-death struggles had taken place.

A war had happened here. Brief, violent, final. A massacre while we'd hidden in the jungle and on the beach, trading with Coo-Hatch and arguing amongst ourselves.

"Ghost town," I whispered. It did that to you. It made you whisper.

"It is quiet," Jalil agreed.

We walked, our sneaks almost noiseless. Hands on our weapons, ready, ready to be jumped by ghosts if nothing else. Ready, scared, relieved. Guilty to be feeling relieved because this was a disaster, this was a horror, a battle involving civilians, not right, but I didn't care what had happened, didn't care what the Vikings had done.

The man-eaters, the heart-thieves, the hungry, ruthless, desperate children of Huitzilopoctli were gone.

We were silent. Our footsteps seemed too loud, advertisements to any that still lived and might attack, a desecration of the many who had surely died.

I don't know if it was deliberate or not, but we were making for the pyramid. I guess it was inevitable. I guess it was what we had to see, to be sure. When we'd seen her, Senna, she'd been near the pyramid.

The pyramid was the heart of this city. If anything still lived and had not run away, it would be there.

And if we found her, what then? "Hey, Senna, what's happening?" What do you say to a witch?

The pyramid was still as it had been. I'd already seen way too much of that foul pile of rocks. I'd see more of it in my nightmares, of that I was sure. I could feel the thing sitting down deep inside my brain, curled up like a rattlesnake in my unconscious mind, ready to strike when I was vulnerable. I knew, knew absolutely that I would climb those steps and watch the bodies slump and the blood trickle, and feel my own heart beating behind my ribs, beating so hard because it wanted to stay alive, didn't want to be torn out, didn't . . .

I stopped and took a couple of deep breaths. Only then did I realize we'd all stopped walking. It was like some invisible force field had frozen us. We stood, a disorderly gaggle of kids from a different universe, looking up through fear-dark eyes at the home office of evil.

"She'll be in the temple," David said.

"If she's here at all," April said.

"How do we know that?" Jalil asked.

"Where else?" April sneered. "Where else but at the middle of it all? Where she's been from the start. Where else, hiding in some burned-out house? No. If anything's alive in this place, it's up there."

"I guess I don't need to point out that something else might be alive up there," I said.

David shook his head "No. Big H is gone. I'd bet on that."

I felt it, too. The sense of emptiness. Abandonment. The sense that people had just gotten up and left at a run, left the blood baking dry on the pyramid steps.

Could Huitzilopoctli's people be gone and Huitzilopoctli remain? It was almost a philosophical question. Maybe someday I'd lay it on Jalil. Show him I did occasionally think beyond the next meal, the next girl, the next joke.

"You know what?" I said. "We climb that stupid pyramid or we never get past this."

"She's up there, waiting, thinking maybe we'll come back and get her. Rescue her. Or she moved out with the others." David squinted up into the sun that seemed to be resting on the temple roof. He started to climb.

"Careful," I muttered. "Don't slip on the blood."

We climbed. I won't say I was as scared as I'd been the first time I went up that pyramid. I don't think I'll ever be that scared again. Lord, I hope not.

But I was scared. Scared enough.

Up we went. Quiet, mostly. An occasional word or remark that died instantly, swallowed up, muffled by the crushing silence.

We topped the platform. The temple now loomed above us. The altar, the black stone operating table, blood-caked six, eight inches thick all around it, years of sun-cooked blood encrusted on it. I wanted dynamite. I wanted to blow it up. Make gravel out of it.

"Look," Jalil said. He pointed. There was a hole through the back of the temple. A hole big enough for a man to jump through. Sunlight blazed through the hole. "I'm guessing Mjolnir."

The inside of the temple was still shadowed but now, with the Viking remodeling job, it was a bit less of a pit.

A noise.

"What was that?" April whispered urgently.

The four of us crouched. I don't know what

kept me from pelting back down that pyramid. We crouched. I gripped my ax. The ax would be useful if Huitzilopoctli came out of that temple. Yeah. About as useful as a feather would be for stopping a Doberman.

Another noise. Like someone had accidentally kicked a can. Not a frightening noise. Except for the fact that no noise is innocent when every nerve in your body is stretched as tight as a guitar string.

"Probably a rat," Jalil said.

"Come on," David said. But he didn't move.

"Oh, after you, General. I insist."

David took a deep breath and started walking like a burglar hoping to fake out the motion sensors. The three of us were right behind him.

From brilliant sunlight into shadow. My eyes took a moment to adjust.

Nothing to see. Mostly emptiness. Some humongous stone platforms, tall and massive as marble mausoleums. Maybe Huitzilopoctli's bed or whatever, who could tell? Some pots. A table.

A man.

CHAPTER
XXVIII

He was rummaging through a sort of shelf inset in one wall. There were earthen jars arrayed neatly, unbroken.

He was tall. Thin, as well as I could tell, given that he was wearing a sort of blue robe or cape.

He spun, surprised. He flicked aside his robe. His hand went instantly to the hilt of a sword hanging in a scabbard. His eyes darted to our weapons, then back to us. He took a quick survey. Then he relaxed.

First impression: He reminded me of my uncle George, an English professor at U of I.

He had blond hair, scruffy, long, dry. The man needed conditioner. His beard and mustache were going gray, giving him overall a sort of greasy, seen-better-times look.

The eyes were intelligent: blue, quick, sunken deep beneath a heavy, lined brow.

He nodded, surprised we were there but not surprised by us. Like he was expecting us, only not here, not now. Like maybe we'd been supposed to meet him later at a coffee shop, and here we were on his front porch.

"Can I help you?" he asked.

I stifled a laugh. Then I stifled an urge to say, "Yeah, party of four and we'd like a booth."

"We're um . . ." David looked at me for guidance. I shrugged.

"We're looking for a friend," April said.

"Indeed?"

"Yes. Yes, indeed."

"I doubt your friend is here. And I doubt that anyone here is your friend," the man said. He shook his head regretfully.

He was blowing us off. Sorry, no one here, maybe you could try back later, now take off because I have things to do. No need for us to waste each other's time any longer, ta-ta.

April was no more interested in being blown off than I was. "We're looking for someone named Senna. Senna Wales."

The man's shrewd eyes were just a bit too indifferent.

"Yes, well, as I said, there's no one here."

"Senna Wales," David pressed. "Our age. Blond hair. Pale eyes."

"A witch," I added dryly.

"For the third, and one can only hope last time, there is no one else here but me, and him."

"Him?"

I looked left. Right. Nothing. Then, slowly, like some horror-movie extra doing a slow take, I looked up. Up to the central mass, the mausoleum-sized table.

My eyes had adjusted to the dark now. And now I could see him.

My knees just gave way. I fell. Kneeling. My heart stopped. Couldn't breathe. No. No. Couldn't be.

He was there. Sitting cross-legged, gigantic, leaning back against the wall of the temple, eyes dark and dull.

Huitzilopoctli.

No one moved. No one breathed. No heart beat.

Then the man in the blue robe laughed. "Don't worry. He's harmless enough at the moment. Well-fed. Overfed."

The man half-twisted to take a critical look upward. "A very stupid god, really. A war god, of course. The gods of war usually are rather dull."

"Is he dead?" April asked.

"No, no. Sadly, no. But injured. And sated. He's a predator, of course. It's all hunger with him. Once he's fed he isn't capable of much beyond sitting and digesting and waiting till the hunger sends him out once more to demand slaughter."

"The people all left," I said.

"Yes, of course. The Norsemen made the city uncomfortable, didn't they? And the people here are starving, so off they've gone to make war on Quetzalcoatl. They need captives, don't they? Prisoners? Fresh hearts for this foul beast of theirs."

His tone had been tolerant, even amused, till the last few words. Then some dark anger had risen to the surface.

"Can he be killed?" Jalil asked.

The man's bemused tone was back. "Oh, Ka Anor will kill him eventually." He turned back to us, smiling. "But then, Ka Anor will kill us all, won't he?"

I shook my head. "Don't ask me, man, I'm just passing through."

The man did not find me amusing. The look he gave me was disappointed. Again he reminded me of my uncle. And most of my teachers.

"We're looking for Senna," David said.

"I wish you well."

"Do you know where she is, yes or no?" Jalil snapped impatiently.

The man laughed. "Do you always show such disrespect for your elders?"

"He asked you a question," David said.

"I have suffered indignities in my long life," the man said. "But I have never before suffered the indignity of being cross-examined by ignorant youths. Youths with no more sense than to come wandering into the temple of Huitzilopoctli."

I laughed. "You know, the thing is, old man, we met Huitzilopoctli earlier, when he was still hungry. Scared the hell out of us." I shot a nervous glance at the dozing blue monster. "Still scares the hell out of me. But you? You're not him, and we've been scared by the best in the business, so you'll have to do better than wiggle the big eyebrows at us if you expect us to run off with our tails between our legs."

Then he laughed. A big, hearty haw-haw-haw laugh. His eyes squinched up small and blue. And nothing about that laugh reached into those cool, calculating eyes.

"Well spoken," he said. "Well spoken, youngster."

He stopped laughing as suddenly as he'd begun. "You may do. You may well do. But for whose purpose, and to what end? Perhaps the witch chose well. And then again, perhaps the witch has outsmarted herself, eh?"

He took a last look at us, turned, and walked away. Jalil was between him and the stairs.

"Hey! Uh-uh, you don't walk away," Jalil protested. He stepped up to grab the old man, but Jalil stopped moving very suddenly.

The rock of the temple floor had grown up and over Jalil's feet. It flowed like lava, then hardened instantly. He was locked, unable to move. A man who'd stood too long in wet cement.

"Son of a —" Jalil yelled.

David ran, sword high, trying to block the old man's way. Suddenly the animal-skin cape David had worn since we escaped from Loki came alive. The fur wrapped around his front and squeezed. David's sword arm was drawn down. He twisted, trying to free himself, fell, rolled. He was no longer a threat to the old man.

I could see the way this was going. I didn't move. April and I exchanged a wary look. This guy, this answer-a-question-with-a-question character in front of us, Huitzilopoctli behind us.

David's clothes became clothes again but he didn't renew his attack.

Jalil whipped out his Coo-Hatch Army knife and sliced at the rock.

The old man saw this and nodded approvingly. "Coo-Hatch steel. It's quite wonderful. I believe they could turn base metal into gold, given the motivation."

"Excuse me, listen, please," April said. "No one wants to annoy you, no one wants you mad at them, we seem to have enough people trying to hurt us, one way or another, but please, please."

He stopped. Smiled. "Please what? Do you have a question?"

April spread her hands placatingly. "Sir, whoever you are, we want to know where we can find Senna. And even more we want to find the way home, back to our universe."

The man considered. Looked at each of us in turn. He was weighing something. Wondering. Concerned. "Never use another man's tools," he muttered under his breath. "Or woman's."

"Will you help us?" April pleaded.

He smiled again, charmed I would almost have thought. "Three questions. Will I help? Perhaps. Where is the witch? Gone. To what place, I do not know. How do you find your home? Home is not found, it is made."

"Great. Runaround." I jerked a thumb at the

man. "Who is this guy? Hey, dude, if you won't help us, at least tell us: Who are you?"

"I've had many names down across the ages, and none of them are any of your business. But I would not be terribly surprised if we were to meet again, so for the sake of polite discourse in the future I'll overlook your present impertinence."

"What'd he say?" I whispered.

The man turned his back on us and stepped off the edge of the platform, down the steps, and out of sight.

"Call me Merlin," a voice said.

A voice only, because by the time we had run to the edge of the platform, the old man was gone from sight.

We followed him soon. We waited for only one reason. The big blue deity of death. It seemed wrong to leave him there. Alive. Alive to enslave his people and murder everyone else.

But there are limits to what a mere mortal can do. Lesson Number One in Everworld: There's them, and there's us. And any day we can keep them from destroying us, that's a victory.

CHAPTER XXIX

"Merlin," I said. "Of course. Why not Merlin, that's the question? Why not the Keebler elves? Why not the Lucky Charms guy, Magically Delicious."

April squinted at me. "That's not his name. You know that, right? His name is not Magically Delicious."

"Hey, wait ten minutes and he'll show up and tell us his name himself," I ranted.

We were on the road, heading out of New Tenochtitlan, following the path the Aztecs had taken, marching through the heat and humidity, along a jungle-crowded trail. Why? Because we were looking for Senna, that's why.

And why were we looking for Senna? Because no one had any better plan.

Or as David put it, "What's the alternative? Go looking for the nearest House of Pancakes?"

"No, we make our own little twenty-first century, U.S. of A. enclave. We wander from place to place like the Coo-Hatch, only we don't obsess over steel, we obsess over the Internet and the economy and the music industry. We go from town to town babbling about our favorite web sites."

"We're going to starve, you realize that," Jalil said. "We're following behind an entire city's worth of hungry people. They'll strip everything, like army ants. There's not going to be a banana peel or a mango seed within a mile either side of this path. Let alone a pig or a . . . a whatever else"

"I guess that means the Aztecs will starve, too," April pointed out.

David sent her a strange look. "They brought their food."

"What? What food? I thought everyone was saying how hungry they were."

I took a certain ghoulish pleasure in filling her in. "The bodies, April. All the dead Aztecs and Vikings? They're just so much jerky now."

We were all quiet for a while after that. Quiet but for the rumbling in our stomachs. Water wasn't so bad a problem. The path seemed to have been cut close to a stream. We could see crushed vegetation where the Aztecs had left the path to grab a drink.

But hunger will get to you pretty quickly. It nags at you. And when nagging doesn't work, it starts yelling. Demanding. Hectoring. Screaming, "Feed me, you moron, I'm starving here!"

"Hey," I said. "What if we go to sleep? Maybe we can eat on the other side and feel full here."

Jalil cocked an eyebrow. He thought it over. Then shook his head in disgust. "That's how hungry I am. I'm starting to actually consider ideas like that."

"At least we'd have the sensation of eating. The memory," I said.

Quiet. Feet on dirt, tripping on rocks and roots. The sound of our own panting breath.

Then April said, "Bibim Bop at the Blind Faith. Carrot cake for dessert."

I made a face. "Bibim Bop? What is that, some vegetarian rabbit food? Keep it basic. Pair of Gold Coast dogs with the works: mustard, onion, chopped tomato, big fat slice of dill pickle, hot peppers, celery salt."

"No ketchup?" David asked.

"Heathen. No. No ketchup on a dog. Mustard, man. Ketchup is for fries. Jeez, how long have you been in Chicagoland, anyway? There's guys at Wrigley Field who'll hurt you over that."

"This is so not helpful," Jalil said angrily. "Talking about food does not help hunger go away. Besides, dogs? That's what you come up with? We're starving, so April wants some vegetarian mush and you want a tube filled with ground-up pig snouts or whatever? That's just sad."

"Okay, Jalil. Let's hear yours," April said tolerantly.

"Best meal I ever had. Best meal anyone ever had. My dad gets promoted, right, big raise and all, so he's feeling like Bill Gates. So he says, 'Hey, let's all get a great meal. Let's get the best meal. The ultimate meal. Charlie Trotter's.'"

"What's a Charlie Trotter? That some kind of horse meat?" David asked.

"Charlie Trotter's, man, it's this restaurant down in Lincoln Park. You don't even order, okay? They bring you everything they have that night. Scallops and chicken and veal and —"

"You shouldn't eat veal," April interrupted.

"— goose liver —"

"You shouldn't eat goose liver, either."

"— just one dish after another, till you can't believe it, man. Just more and more, better and better."

"I'd eat a goose head right now, let alone a goose liver," David said. "I would eat some Aztec jerky about now. Although, what I really want?

Breakfast. I'll eat breakfast any time of the day. Eggs. Over medium. Bacon. Home fries."

"You like the onion in the home fries or not?" April asked.

He shook his head. "No. Just potatoes. Rye toast. Can't always get it, but I like rye toast with just the butter. No jelly. Yeah. Mop up the eggs with that."

He sighed. We all sighed. And the sun slid down toward the horizon.

"What do we do when it gets dark?" I asked.

"We talk about dessert," April said.

CHAPTER XXX

Night seemed to take forever to come, but when it came at last, it dropped like a midnight-blue curtain. The sky filled with stars. Fewer stars than we'd have seen in the wilderness back in our world, but brighter, larger, nearer. Not like far-off suns burning atomic fires. More like the sky was a big, black bowl slammed down over us, shutting out the light of day except for here and there where someone had bored holes in the bowl. You felt like you were looking at buttery, warm sunlight peeking through a thousand tiny ratholes.

Who knows? In this place, maybe that was true.

The hungry walk had been depressing enough. Night didn't turn it into a party.

"Better find a place to pull off and catch some

Z's," David said, when at last we could no longer clearly see our feet on the trail.

"Not yet," April said.

"Why not? You in a hurry to get somewhere?"

She took David's head from behind with both her hands and pointed it. "There. You see something?"

"What?" Jalil demanded.

"A light."

"Campfire?" David speculated.

Jalil said, "Group of Aztecs most likely. Or else thieves."

"Or else trolls or goblins or leprechauns or fairies or magic flying pigs," I muttered.

"Maybe they have food," David said.

"Maybe the food they have isn't exactly something we want to eat," April said pointedly.

"Never eat anything with a face?" I joked.

"At least not a human face."

"Ouch."

"It's a simple question," David said. "Either we go in or we hide. I —" He started to add something else, then stopped himself. "What do you guys think?"

"What do you know? General Patton pauses to consult the privates," I said. "Okay, we go in. IMHO. Because if we don't find some food, we are gonna be food. And if we starve we can't sleep and we can't even go home and eat back in the real world."

"Approach with caution, I'd say." That was Jalil.

"I need a weapon, I don't have one," April said. Then, to David, mocking, "See? Was that so hard? Ask people."

"Give the woman Excalibur, Jalil," I suggested.

He handed her the tiny knife. She gave it a skeptical look. "Hey, I bet I could shave my legs with this."

"Yeah, down to the bone. Be careful with it."

"Okay. We move in, surround the fire," David said, Patton once more. "One goes in all innocent, the other three spread wide, come in from three separate angles. The one who walks in is on the spot."

"Let's have four coins," April said. "We flip till we get three of one, odd-person-out walks in with a big smile."

"I knew there'd be some use for this money," I said.

We flipped. First time, it was me with tails. Three heads and my tails.

"Best two out of three?" I joked.

David looked hard at me, like he was sizing me up for the mission. Man, I was getting to really dislike him.

"Give us twenty minutes to get into position," he said.

"Yeah, no problem. I'll just sit here and play a few rounds of solitaire."

"First sign of trouble, yell. We'll be all over the place. If it's obviously trouble, you know, a bunch of guys, something we can't take down, back off fast. Yell if they come after you, we'll give you cover."

I laughed. "David, do you understand it's just you, Jalil, and April? You understand there's no artillery to call in for cover, right? I mean, unless you've been holding out on us and you secretly have a troop of cavalry back in the jungle over there, it's just the three of you."

He grinned. I could see his teeth and the whites of his eyes. "We escaped from Loki, we rocked with the Vikings, we beat Huitzilopoctli. Who's up there by that fire that we can't handle?"

"I guess we'll find out in about twenty minutes," I said.

They left. David to the left of the trail, Jalil and April to the right. I could hear them thrashing around. Then, gradually, silence.

I stared hard through the darkness, stared at the faint fire, if that's what it was. Pictured some old black-and-white movie — maybe they were hobos, that's what they called them back in the old days. Hobos. Bums. Sitting around a campfire warming a can of beans.

Or maybe it was Girl Scouts. I forced a smile for my own benefit. What did they call the older Girl Scouts? Explorers? Was that it? A troop of high-school-aged Girl Scouts, that was it, working on their merit badges in Hospitality to Strange Men.

Maybe they'd have cookies. Thin Mints. I'd take the beans or the cookies, I could go either way.

Hard to hold on to those pleasant fantasies, though. Those images were made out of air. The other fantasies were flesh and blood. Renegade Aztec warriors. Loki's trolls. Some other bunch of aliens.

Hey! Maybe it was the Coo-Hatch. Yeah, that was it. Coo-Hatch. They were okay, they were cool. Weird but not violent, at least not so far.

Or maybe it was the guy who called himself Merlin. You could talk to him at least. Probably wouldn't eat us. Probably wouldn't kill us; he could have done that if he'd wanted.

Twenty minutes? Was the time up yet? How was I supposed to know?

"Close enough," I muttered. "No point hanging around wondering. Come on, old son, march."

I started toward the fire. Not a happy walk.

It's never a party when you're walking through darkness, utter darkness, when every weed that brushes your arm is the reaching hand of a monster.

"Man, this so chews," I said, talking to keep myself from running. "Like I could run. Where would I run?"

You'd think it would be easier to be brave when you know you don't have an alternative. But I wasn't finding that to be true.

Closer. Walking. Then creeping. Tiptoeing. Holding my breath, cursing the noise of my rumbling stomach. I was gonna get killed for being hungry. Maybe they had food. Cookies. Beans. A nice leg o' human.

The fire was definitely fire. Small. That was good. It was a fire built for one or two, maybe three. Not a whole army.

Closer. Pushing the leaves aside, trying to see what there was to see. A hint of something near the fire. Couldn't see. Eyes straining, aching from the squint, head pounding now with the tension.

I was lower, hunched over. *Don't see me, don't see me. Let me see you, but don't see me.*

No! This was wrong. Whatever was out here in the middle of nowhere might be scared, too. Jumpy and armed, a bad combination. If I crept up, snuck, seemed to be attacking, it was all over.

No, David was right: big smile, innocent look,
arms wide.

I sucked in wet air. I stood up. I walked on wobbly legs.

I stepped into a clearing. A neat, circular space,
walled by close-packed bushes and saplings and
weeds.

In the center, a small fire.

Sitting by the fire, legs crossed, arms resting
palms up, face worried, eyes staring into the fire,
was Senna Wales.

CHAPTER XXXI

"You!" I snapped.

"Christopher?" she said, sounding for all the world like I was exactly, precisely the person she'd been waiting for, hoping for.

I didn't have anything brilliant to say after "you." I didn't have anything to say at all. We'd been looking for Senna, but now that she was sitting, apparently calmly, by a cheerful little fire, none of it seemed real.

I'd been ready for trolls or elves or Loki's big nasty son, Fenrir, the gigantic wolf. I'd been ready for Coo-Hatch or Merlin or one of Ka Anor's strange, half-insect people. I'd been ready for monsters. Not for her.

She waited expectantly, ready to listen to what I had to say.

"You have any food?" I asked. "I'd trade my left arm for a bag of Doritos and some salsa."

She nodded thoughtfully. "Yes. I have food. Not Doritos. But I have some little cakes."

Once again, the conversation died. She said nothing else. Just waited. Like this whole thing was my idea and she was my guest, waiting to see if I had any new activities planned.

I couldn't see her as Senna. Not the Senna I'd known. Too much had happened. I knew too much, and suspected more.

"You know, I really want to thank you for bringing me to this party," I said. "So far I've been hung from Loki's castle walls, chased, half-drowned, had to sing the "Battle Hymn of the Republic" to keep from being killed by drunken Vikings, hunted by crazy Aztecs, and almost had my heart cut out and fed to a big blue god. So, as vacations go, this one is great."

Senna said nothing in direct response. I'm pretty sure she detected the note of sarcasm in my voice. She'd have had to be deaf not to detect the note of sarcasm.

She leaned to one side and opened a sort of shoulder bag I hadn't noticed before. She withdrew a parcel wrapped in green leaves. Within the leaf wrapping, a small round cake.

She handed it over, I took it, our fingers touched accidentally. I felt a charge. Excitement. A rush.

I stuffed the cake in my mouth. It tasted like corn bread.

Then I yelled, "Okay, you guys, it's okay."

"The others are alive?" Senna asked. A polite question. Sort of like, "And how is your grandmother doing after the surgery?"

"Oh, yeah, we're all fine. Time of our lives, Senna. We all love it here at the Everworld Club Med. It'll be a shame when we have to go home."

I swear I wanted to slap her. Not a glimmer of guilt. Nothing.

"You don't happen to know how we do that, I guess? Go home, I mean. North? South? Take a left at the first lunatic god and go past three elves? Do we take the troll road?"

That brought a faint smile.

Then David stepped into the firelight. He stopped and stared at her. Not a happy stare. It was too complex for that. I swear the first expression that crossed his face was disappointment.

I don't know what I expected from David. I wouldn't have been surprised if he'd yelled, "Oh, baby!" and run to her arms. Disappointment? Why? Didn't like her outfit?

Ah, no, no, of course. David was worried that maybe the big adventure was all over. Me, I was worried it wasn't.

Neither of them said anything. But I could tell Senna was disappointed in her own way. I had a feeling maybe she was looking for the big Hallmark moment, too. Expecting her little love puppy to come bounding over and lay his head down on her lap to have his ears scratched.

"Hello, David."

He nodded. Said nothing.

Then Jalil and April emerged into the light. Jalil went into cautious mode. He knew, just like I did, that the Big Show, the Main Event, was between David and Senna. He was hanging back, waiting to listen and understand.

April didn't hang back. She walked straight to Senna, stopped, leaned down, drew back her right hand, and nailed Senna with a slap that echoed against the trees.

The two girls stared at each other. Fury from April. And what from Senna? Not rage. Not guilt or remorse. Not fear, certainly.

Arrogance. That was it. The calm, superior, sneering look of the two-hundred-and-fifty-pound linebacker who's just been punched by the ninety-five-pound gymnast. The look said, "Go ahead, slap me again. I'll crush you in my own good time."

I guess April saw the look the same why I did. She didn't repeat the slap.

"You were happy enough to see me when I brought you weapons to escape Huitzilopoctli," Senna said.

"I can be ruthless, too, sister. I needed you then."

"So. You guys all know each other, right?" I said, breaking the ensuing silence. "Senna, that's David, April, and Jalil. Everybody? I'd like you all to meet Senna. The witch. She brought cake! A very nice gesture, I'd say."

CHAPTER XXXII

We sat down. We ate corn cake.

Of all the many weird moments we'd encountered since we made the mistake of going down to Lake Michigan early one morning, this was one of the oddest.

Odd because it had such a superficial normalcy. Odd because we each had a million questions, so many questions no one seemed to know where to start.

Fortunately, that's why Jalil is good to have around. He knew where to start.

"You going to tell us what this is all about, Senna?"

"What all of it is about? Who can ever answer that?"

Jalil was unimpressed. "You can. And you know, I don't want to hear a bunch of metaphysical 'who can say?' b.s., so how about you start at the beginning and tell us what you're doing getting snatched off the pier by a mythical wolf and hauled into this alternate universe."

"You ask for simple answers to questions that even the wisest of the wise would —"

"Senna, cut the crap," Jalil snapped.

Senna's eyes went wide. David tensed involuntarily and shot Jalil a dangerous look.

Me? I could have kissed him. Exactly! Cut the crap. Answer the question. Final Jeopardy, Senna the Witch.

"I knew I would be taken," Senna said. "I had been resisting it for some time, but I knew eventually my resistance would fail. I knew it might endanger people near me when it happened. I found an isolated place and time, and allowed it to happen."

"Next question," I prompted Jalil.

"Fenrir was supposed to take you to Loki. What happened?"

Senna shrugged. "Loki is very clever. He is not all-powerful."

"Where did you go?" Jalil asked.

"Why bring us here with you?" David asked.

Senna chose David's question. "I didn't. That was an accident."

April snorted. "David told us how you asked

him to save you, protect you. You set this all up. We're not total idiots, Senna, although I know that's what you've always thought. Ever since we were kids and you . . ."

She stopped. Senna smirked. "Ever since what, April?"

Silence. They glared, eye to eye. Then April looked away. A red flush darkened her face.

Senna looked from one of us to the next, holding each of us in turn with her dark stare. "If you follow your fate, don't blame me because your path and mine run together."

"I'm still getting gibberish here," Jalil said. "I don't need this Tolkien-lite, pseudoprofound nonsense. I want more of that, I can go back and find what's his name. Merlin."

Senna jerked violently. I took a step back. It was like she'd been stabbed or something. Like she'd been bitten by a snake. I was looking for attackers, back up, head turning, adrenaline flooding into my muscles.

"Merlin," she whispered.

Suddenly I liked the old man a lot more. I liked the fact that the mention of his name could wipe the smug, know-it-all look off Senna's face.

She stood up, started left, stopped, started right. Stopped. She wrung her hands. Literally

"What did you tell him?" she demanded.

Jalil was liking this, too. "We told him we were looking for you, Senna."

Her face was pale in the golden firelight. "Do you think this is funny? Do you think Merlin is some feeble old man? I knew an attack was coming, I felt it, but from him? From Merlin?"

"An attack?" Suddenly David was alert and ready, grabbing the hilt of his sword.

Senna went to him and cradled his face with one hand. David blinked. "Save me, David," she said. "Save me, or he will kill us all."

She looked deep into David's glazed eyes. Nodded, like she was satisfied.

Then she came for me. I flinched. She smiled. A forced, hurried smile. She was trying to be unthreatening. Trying to look like the girl I'd thought I was falling for once. A shark with a big give-me-a-hug grin.

She put her hand on my face. I pulled away. No. No, I didn't pull away. Couldn't.

My mind flooded with images, memories. Senna, as I'd first seen her. Senna kissing me. Senna touching . . . Senna . . .

"Fight for me, Christopher. Be brave and defend me."

Her hand was gone. I was alone. But the enemy was coming! I had to save her. Had to try, had to try.

Swiftly she moved toward Jalil.

But then, above the soft wind-shushing of the trees, came a larger sound. Wind like a tornado. Louder and louder. Nearer.

Up. It was coming from above. Not from the jungle. Flying above the jungle just above the treetops.

It glowed against the night sky. It glowed like a coal when you blow on it. Like the red light that shines from within the flowing magma.

It was so big. A bird, but no, of course it wasn't a bird. No bird could ever be this big. No bird would fly with the sound of leather sliding over bone, no bird released the tornado with each downstroke.

A hundred feet from wingtip to wingtip. Longer still from its forked, whipping tail to its horned head. Teeth that were three feet long. Teeth clearly outlined, black against the liquid fire that ran like vomit from its mouth and left brushfires in its wake.

Senna quailed. Drew back from Jalil.

But even as she drew back I saw her face, just for a moment, a vision illuminated by the dragon's fire. A smile. A killer's smile, as though the lips might stretch still further and reveal vampire fangs.

She was afraid. But she was greedy, too. Hungry

for some chance that grew more possible with the approach of the beast.

I saw all this. And knew that this was not my fight. That Senna was not mine to protect. But my mind was no longer entirely mine to command. And my skepticism, my understanding evaporated, burned away by Senna's touch.

She turned and looked up at the monster. The dragon saw her. Its yellow cat's eyes glittered. Yellow wings beat the air, rustling the bushes, bowing the saplings. Talons spread wide, ready to grapple.

No need to fear, Senna, my mind said. *No need. I'll save you. I'll kill it, Merlin's monster.*

I'll kill the dragon.

EVER WORLD

#III
ENTER THE ENCHANTED

I was far from home.

As far from home as it is possible for a human being to get. Not a far place, a place apart, a place not touching reality, isolated.

Forget the normal. Normal was gone. Normal belonged to the real world.

There was magic here. Not magic like "ah, the moonlight was magic." Magic as in cause and effect didn't always cause or effect. The magic that negates all human knowledge, that invalidates ten thousand years of human learning.

Usually gravity worked, sometimes not. No way for that to be, of course, gravity isn't something you can turn on or off, if it was it wouldn't be gravity. If gravity could come and go, wax and wane, then things could fly when they could not possibly fly.

Like a dragon, maybe.

Can't possibly lift something as heavy and dense as a dragon, all that scaly skin, all that muscle, all that dense bone, not with wings, not with leathery wings like a pterodactyl. Wings that were not a tenth of what they had to be, not a hundredth of what was needed to raise this creature, this logic-killing monster into the air.

An elephant with wings! Dumbo, but not cute.

And fire. Could fire burn inside a living creature? Absurd. Ridiculous. Fire inside what, the belly? The intestines? The liver? Liquid flame spilling out of flesh, out of the monster's mouth, and that was supposed to be real? That was happening?

I stood, rooted, yes rooted, like my toes had grown down into the dirt looking for water and now I couldn't move them because my feet were attached to the earth itself, or whatever passed for Earth in this hideous, terrible place.

Run? How could I run from the dragon who pressed the tall trees down with the wind from his impossible wings and flamed the dry bushes in the night?

I could only stare. A miracle, that's what it was. A dragon.

"Damn it, April, run!" Jalil yelled.

His face was wild, not like Jalil, eyes wide, mouth stretched into some indecipherable shape, half grin, half howl.

Only Jalil cared. About me. And that, not much. David and Christopher were mesmerized, bewitched. More magic. She had gone to them, touched them, spoken to them, and they had lost themselves.

They stood with pitiful swords drawn, defiant and foolish, waving their impotent weapons up at the killer from the sky.

Jalil grabbed me, pulled me, dragged me. My feet moved, missed a step, tripped, up again, and now I ran. But not far. I had to stop, to see.

"Go back to your master, Merlin! Tell him I am not his!" Senna screamed. Her voice was a tinny, faraway shout, a sound all but erased by the vastness of the noise, the howling wind, the bellows sigh of leather wings, the crackle of underbrush bursting into flame.

The dragon inscribed slow, tight circles above the clearing, a living tornado, flying like a bird of prey, an eagle with green and yellow skin, with talons that could carry away a child, a man, a horse, what couldn't it carry with gravity meaningless?

Jalil and I huddled in the woods, unprotected by bowed trees and whipped grass and dirt flying in little cyclones. But the dragon didn't care for us. It watched Senna.

Have her! Take her! I cried silently. This is her nightmare.